Sacred Jewel Within

Li-Ing Wu

Publisher: Inspiring Publishers,
P.O. Box 159, Calwell,
ACT Australia 2905
Email: publishaspg@gmail.com
http://www.inspiringpublishers.com

National Library of Australia The Prepublication Data Service

Author: Li-Ing Wu

Title: Sacred Jewel Within

Genre: Non-fiction

ISBN: 978-1-925908-55-8 (print)
      978-1-925908-56-5 (ePub2)
      978-1-925908-57-2 (eBook)

Exclusion of Liability

Table of Contents

Foreword

I am a firm believer that everything happens for a reason and nothing is by chance. One might say my meeting Li-Ing was providential. We share a common purpose in our desire to serve humanity.

When conversing with Li-Ing, her desire to help sentient beings break free from their limiting self-beliefs and reclaim their Divinity is apparent.

Li-Ing shares her innate wisdom in <u>Sacred Jewel Within</u> to help you shed unnecessary perceived burdens and develop a greater self-understanding, self-empowerment and personal growth in your life.

You've picked up this book because you are seeking more; from life and from yourself. You are seeking the freedom to live the life of your dreams and your purpose. <u>Sacred Jewel Within</u> does exactly that. It helps one uncover one's own underlying truth as each chapter unveils another level of unconscious conditioning as you work through each chapter and do the 'homework'.

<u>Sacred Jewel Within</u> is not just another self help book. This book is your guide to help uncover behavioural patterns, limiting self-beliefs and blocks; some of which you may not even be aware.

This book intends to help bridge the gap between one's higher self and one's physical being. We truly have the potential to create Heaven or Hell on this Earth, so we may as well make it Heaven. <u>Sacred Jewel Within</u> enables you to live a life connected with your higher self so that everyday feels like Heaven.

I encourage you to use this book as a reference guide and workbook. Come back to it as many times as you need, there is no limit to your potential and <u>Sacred Jewel Within</u> will help guide you back home to yourself.

Once you begin on your self-development journey turn your face towards the sun and keep going. If you take the old saying "one can choose to go back toward the safety of one's comfort zone or forward towards growth", I say choose growth. The comfort zone may feel like a beautiful place, however nothing ever grows there.

Embrace the journey you are about to embark upon, it will truly change your life.

Aida Jasmine,
Spiritual Intuitive, Healer and Teacher

Author's Note

In the Western societies, perhaps it is due to the Roman Empire's political and spiritual manipulations to alter the Bible in the 4th century (325 A.D.); or rather, it's due to our over-emphasis of the rationalism, reductionist approach, and misuse of Darwin's evolution theory, we have "thrown away the baby (the belief in spirituality) along with the bath water (the blind faith in religion and superstitions) over the last few centuries. We have adapted a very analytical, microscopic, mechanistic and competitive approach to literally all aspects of life. Everything has to be broken down to smaller and smaller fragments for rational analysis. It is so much so, that the famous American systemic physicist and ecology activist Fritjof Capra (1975) once said that we all are specialists in life, but lacked the overall inter-dependent, inter-connecting views of how each component interacts as a whole. Our excessive obsessions with materialism, high technology, consumptions and ego-based pursuits in life are good glimpses to our rather off-balanced evolution as a human species.

We are taught that unless matters can be tested or measured by quantity in a concrete way with consistent results, they either are invalid or do not exist. Being "rational" and "scientific"are almost synonyms for "reliable" and "the truth". In many situations, they even surpass "God". Anything considered as beyond reasoning is to be ridiculed or disregarded as nonsense even though not all situations can be tested or proven by the science.

We allow our intellects and reasons to rule us like tyrants. However, rational analysis is but one of the many means (and often, not the most reliable means) of accessing the Universal or Higher Truths. Our intuitions, Extra Sensory Perceptions or the sixth sense are the means of how our Soul Self-communicates with our physical body. In many ways, they can be more effective for devising great innovation and accessing the cosmic truths. Nicola Tesla's ingenuous and humanitarian innovations are great examples of using the 6th senses, and they are centuries ahead of Thomas Edison's. However, with the dominance of rationalism in our education and society, we are discouraged from being in touch with our own soul languages. Our innate direct knowing has long been put aside as "witchcraft", "superstition", "entertainment", "fiction", "airy-fairy" or "laughing stock" for thousands of years until recently.

In our schools and universities, instead of cultivating the basics of human inner essence, values, high ethics, respect, truth, integrity and altruism with the emphasis on cooperation, gratitude, beauty, peace, harmony, benevolence, self-responsibility, empathy and oneness which are more the "feminine" or the "Yin" qualities of life; we pride ourselves with external acquisition, speed, quantity with major focus on the "masculine" or "Yang" aspects of life such as dollar sign, numbers, material possession, competition, greed, power, and dominance. We justify the latter with "the fittest survive" based on our conditioned fears of lack and scarcity instead of trust of abundance with the equal distribution of our wealth for the highest good of all.

With excessive pursuit of everything external of us, we see lots of "materially rich", yet "spiritually–broken" in our global society. Ironically, with all these highly advanced technology and massive computerisation and atomisation, we feel ever more so empty, lonely, and alienated around the globe. We have inherited a beautiful and bountiful earth planet and yet less than 1% of our population get to control the 99% of our wealth. We also are poisoning ourselves and our ecosystem with drugs, pollutants, wastes, chemicals and bombings in a speed that is bringing massive self-destructions like never before. In essence, our "global crisis" in our economy, society and environment is "a crisis of perceptions" (Capra, 2014). Our human civilisation has been much skewed towards the Yang (the masculine principles of life) for too long. It's about time for us to bring back major balance to restore our spiritual wellbeing and fulfilment in life.

Being global citizens, we each as individuals are responsible for what is going on in our community. All changes start from within ourselves. Throughout this book, I am using "we" a lot because literally, we are on this boat of humanity together. In <u>The Butterfly Effect</u>, the author states that we have been created in order that we might make a difference. We have within us the power to change the world (Andrews, 2010).

When I write and intuit this book, my simple wish is to bridge the missing links between our heads and our hearts; our conditioned self and our Soul Self to help humanity. Decades ago, as a shy teenager, I was rather inspired by the Indian yogi Yogananda and his numerous spiritual ventures in the Himalayan Mountains (Yogananda, 1946) as well as the spiritual materials contained in <u>Seth Speaks</u> (Roberts, 1972). Further fascinated by the Taiwanese author Three Hair and her life adventure in Spain and the Sahara Desert (San Mao, 1976), these influences set off my personal spiritual quests to the foreign lands to explore different means of self-empowerment and assistance to humanity. Decades later, I am returning the favour now. We are channels of blessings to one another. I hope to hear your story one day.

Li-Ing Wu 2019 Australia

Acknowledgement

This book is not a pure effort of mine. I want to thank my forever patient and supportive divine angel guidance team first. Although invisible to me, they have given me lots of guidance, support, inspiration and intuitions in my life-long spiritual quest.

Millions of thanks to my loving parents Pine-Forest and Elegant-Orchid who have supported me whole-heartedly, financially, emotionally and spiritually to pursue my dreams through their lifelong's hard work, self-sacrifice and generosity. Not only do they give me wings, they also give me the freedom to fly as high and far as I wish. My gratitude also goes to my older sister Wise-and-Gracious who has taught me deep compassion and honesty through her disability and strong presence in my life. I want to thank my sister Beautiful-Shine-of-Jade who showers me with non-stop emotional and spiritual support along my life's journey and challenges. My gratitude also goes to late Dr. Jon Young from Hawaii, who was my mentor in the art and science of holistic body-mind-spirit healing.

Finally, my gratitude goes to all the others who are closest to me and who have shared the essence of their lives with me. They have provided me ample opportunities to understand the diversity, complexity, and depth of human psyche in many rich contexts as I moved from Asia to America to Australia.

I want to thank you the readers too. Each individual ray contributes towards the sun as a whole. By you taking on this journey of personal growth and self-mastery, you are transforming our humanity already. Many heartfelt thanks to you and congratulations for adding your expression and experience of who you are to enrich our humanity as a whole.

How to Use This Book

This is a hands-on book. It is metaphysical and philosophical in nature but the simple tools and principles contained are rather practical. These presented concepts and devised tools are the results of my life-long soul search, and intuited higher truths. They address common themes faced by humanity. For that I also owe lots of gratitude to many great philosophers, pioneer physicists, mystics, visionaries, angels, Archangels, Ascending Masters, the Highly Evolved Beings and our Great Creator known or unknown to our human world.

The entire book is written in a sequence where one theme builds upon another. Whilst some chapters may stand out to you, I recommend that you go through the whole book chapter by chapter at some stage to ensure that you get the most out of it as a coherent whole. You may go back to a certain chapter to review as a major focus as needed.

When I wrote the book, my intention was to create a hands-on self-help book for your metaphysical self–understanding, self-empowerment and personal growth. There is therefore a small homework at the end of each chapter for you to practise the new concepts in your daily life as deemed suitable by your own best judgements. After all, knowledge without actions is dead. It's only when we apply what we know that we can truly benefit from it. I recommend that you go through each chapter on a weekly or fortnightly basis. The most robust gardens often are the results of dedicated loving care in moderation without over-doing or under-feeding. Once the garden is well-established, its strong life force takes care of itself; we need only sparing care thereafter.

In general, all of the metaphysical concepts and tools presented here are for our personal use. Despite our human systems being far from perfect, it is important to respect human laws much like: "when in Rome, act as the Romans do". Between common sense and idealism, there is always a balance. Thus, my advice is to use our common sense and super sense (intuitions) in a balanced way *to love intelligently and to think lovingly* with self-responsibility and sound judgments when applying these tools for our self-transformation.

In this journey of self-empowerment, we can best serve our humanity by "walking the talk". Let others be naturally inspired and gravitate towards our self-transformation because such modelling is what many of us come in to do to uplift humanity. This is the "ripple effects" I referred to earlier. Whilst we approach life from cosmic perspectives, it is important that we also accept "non-acceptance" by others without taking it personally.

In this journey of expanding our self-knowledge and self-power to a broader horizon, the main thing is to trust that even if there are obstacles along the way, we'd always have the intelligence and needed support to make it through. Even if there are some sidetracks, detours, accidents or emergencies on the road, they are learning curves to train us different kind of intelligence in life and they are of good value. *"Flawlessness", "effectiveness" and "speediness" are human-conditioned signposts for success. However, side-tracks, detours, and emergencies can teach us lessons of faith, tenacity, patience, risk-taking, humility and adaptability etc. which are equally important.* None of them are a waste of time. *The yard stick for success is not based on whether we reach the ultimate goal immediately but rather, to count every step along the journey as "part of the success already". Aiming at "progress" with self-appreciation is always a better way of motivating further progress rather than demanding "perfection" with self-criticism each time.*

Above all, let's have fun and rejoice at every small milestone of our personal growth! The Italians find every excuse to celebrate life. The angels fly because they "take themselves light-heartedly". So can we!

Bon Voyage!

Chapter 1
Sacred Jewel Within

*"Knowing others is intelligence;
knowing yourself is true wisdom.
Mastering others is strength;
mastering yourself is true enlightenment."*
— *Lao Tzu, <u>Tao Te Ching</u>*

I have once come across a beautiful saying which states: "what lies behind us or ahead of us is nothing compared to what lies inside of us". What lies inside of us is our Soul essence, sacred, creative, infinite, divine and eternal. Literally, we are souls having physical bodies, not physical bodies having souls.

Our spirits are the "cause"; the material world and matters are but the "effects". To chase after effect and ignore the cause is like chasing the shadow or mirage. The more we buy into the external chase of "matter over mind" and "materialism above all", the more we grow alienated to the true essence and inner sacred jewels of who we are. I believe that the cultivation of who we truly are as divine eternal multi-dimensional energy beings, and to respect all individuals and species as equal and unseparated as one are what we desperately need at this point to restore the peace, harmony and sustainability on our planet earth.

Great saints, mystics, prophets and philosophers often derive their truths by observing the nature surrounding them or by tuning within for Higher Wisdom. To restore our wellbeing as a species and for all species on earth, it is crucial that we understand the divine nature and divine identity of our Real Self.

As the famous proverb states: "As within, so without; as above, so below". The critical mass can be achieved only if we all turn within to cultivate our innate sacred jewels as the priorities in life. We can also evolve faster as a species by following the footsteps of the exceptional living role-models of the Ascending Masters like Jesus, Mother Mary, Buddha, Babaji and Yoganada; saints like Mother Teresa; and great leaders like Ghandi and Mandela! Whilst we may not serve humanity exactly like them, the willingness to look within ourselves to re-claim and polish our divine jewels of who we are is already grand in itself! The elevation of our raised frequency will benefit our globe as well as many other visible and invisible galaxies and dimensions surrounding and beyond us. The choice is for us to make here and now in each conscious moment of our life.

The pursuit of the infinite spiritual jewels within us does not denote that we should exclude nor ignore our physical and material needs. After all, we are divine beings living in this physical dimension. The point of this book is to pinpoint that *we are in this physical world, but not of it!* Whilst we can fully enjoy our myriad world and phenomenon, becoming over-attached or over-indulged in it sidetracks us from cultivating the far more precious sacred jewel-like divinity we really are. My point is to emphasize the balance between our ego and Soul Self; material pursuit and higher (not necessarily religious) principles; our self's own good with the highest good of all.

Many of us confuse the concept of "spirituality" with "religion". Spirituality is universal, irrelevant of race, age, species, culture, gender, time, location and dimension. It is innate in all of the living things and governs life indefinitely. The ancient Chinese naturalist philosophers (the Taoists) call these universal principles running innate and governing all living things "the Tao" (the Way of Life). Some call it Life, some call it the Great Universe whilst some call it God. Religion, on the other hand, is man-made concepts based on human interpretations which are often manipulated by political power and control to cater for the wellbeing of a few elites.

Humans spend life time after life time chasing the visible jewels in the outside world, holding the illusion that the material wealth and comfort are what life is all about. Few have recognised the far more precious and sacred jewels innate in us. We come in empty-handed and we go back to our Divine Origin empty-handed. We even shed our physical body when we die. Many people wait until the last breath to realise that the only jewels that we are able to take Home with us are the innate sacred jewels we have cultivated and fulfilled in this physical journey. So, why not use such foresights to cultivate our very precious sacred jewel within NOW instead of regretting at our death point?

As we are created in the same essence as our Father / Mother God, what our Father/Mother God is made of and capable of, so are we. The sacred jewels I refer to thus include the same essence of the Source, namely: Love, Joy, Peace, Truth, Freedom, All-Knowing Intelligence, Giving, Benevolence, Kindness, Forgiveness, Gentleness, Perfection, Non-Judgemental Compassion, Creativity, Faith, Abundance, Omnipresence, Omnipotence, Patience etc. (Lanphear, 1987)

As multi-dimensional energy beings, it takes tremendous courage for us to embark in this physical world because it is full of exciting adventures well-designed for our soul growth. Whilst our Soul Selves embodies the Higher Intelligence of Life; our physical selves Express and Experience our greatest version of the grandest vision of our Divine Nature and Identity (Walsh, Neale 2017). We go through the journey in this duality world because "that which is cannot know or experience itself fully, without something it is not" (Neale Walsh, 1995). We inter- depend with our Soul Selves to co-create our reality as individualised selves and as a Collective Whole moment to moment, existence after existence in a forever-evolving and forever-expanding way. Each individual sunray contributes to the totality of the sun's overall expansion and evolvement. Whatever stage we are in, it is nothing short of grandness and magnificence!

Small Homework:

Imagine ourselves being a mine full of precious illuminating jewels. From the jewels of love, kindness, giving, forgiving, patience, integrity, strength, courage, humour, optimism, to jewels of openness, flexibility, adaptability, consideration, empathy to determination and faith etc. etc. Imagine them all as ours unlimited.

*Dig out three different jewels each day and say to the Great Universe, "Thank you for creating me with the essence of ____, ____ and ____". Be grateful to the Universe that you are made of these sacred jewel-like innate qualities. Do embrace these qualities and fully own these qualities and **cherish them from within**. Don't be surprised how many people recognise and appreciate us like jewels when practising this. When people compliment us, say to them, "Thank you! It takes one to know one!"*

Chapter ii

The Conditioning

***"One believes things because
one has been conditioned to believe them."***
*— Aldous Huxley (1894-1963),
a humanist & mysticism philosopher*

In my years of work for humanity, I have observed how our limiting self-concepts and low self-worth affect most aspects of our human life. They impair our general physical wellbeing, relationships with ourselves, significant others and community, money matters, work, career, and level of fulfilment in every turn and corner of our life!

Self-confidence is the foundation to the skyscraper of life

I have also observed how the limiting self-concepts get passed on generation to generation through our moment-to-moment daily routines with familial, educational, social, cultural and public media's conditionings. The built-up repeated contingencies often leave deep imprints in our subconscious mind. It's as if they leave "prototype imprints" with which our subconscious keeps duplicating much like the replays of an old broken record in every stage and at times, every aspect of our life.

Subconscious mind auto-pilots with automatic-response

The subconscious mind often operates in an auto-piloting and automatically-reactive manner whether we are consciously aware or not. Scientific studies have found out that humans have **tens of thousands** of thoughts per day. To be modest, let's say we have 300 thoughts daily as the result of daily interactions with our family of origin.

At the end of one year, we would have accumulated 365 days x 300 thoughts/ day= 109,500 thoughts / year. By the time we leave home at age 20, we would have easily accumulated

2,190,000 repeated thoughts which would form many powerful "core beliefs". Many of these core beliefs may be unpleasant and distressing, thus, our self-defence mechanism would repress or suppress them into our "subconscious mind" beyond our full-on knowing.

These repeated thoughts and images and conditionings constitute the 95% of our mind. The auto-piloting functioning of our subconscious mind means that when our conscious mind is engaged in something else, our subconscious mind will automatically take over by taking us to our most familiar place called the "comfort zone". Ironically, "comfort zones" are not always comfortable; it simply means that we gravitate naturally towards the place where we have been for hundreds of thousands of times.

Subconscious mind takes us to our "comfort zone" when conscious mind is non-attentive

To illustrate, on day one when we first learn to drive a car, our coach says to us, "when the red light is on, make sure your foot is on the brake; when it turns green, make sure your foot hits the accelerator of the car". Initially, when we are not familiar with the car's different parts, we are super conscious to ensure that we and our foot coordinate perfectly with the traffic lights we see. Despite how nervous we are, let's say that it takes 20 traffic lights before we reach our workplace and another 20 traffic lights on the way back. This means that we drive through 40 traffic lights per day. At the end of 2 months, this means we will be driving through 2400 traffic lights! Day in and day out, red light (brake); green light (accelerator): red light (brake); green light (accelerator); red light (brake), green light (accelerator) constant pairing and contingency repeats for 2,400 times, the conditionings of such link of "stimulus- response" has quickly become our "comfort zone" which also goes to our subconscious mind. Two months later, we may be driving on the way to work with our conscious mind pre-occupied with the plan of our best friend's wedding; however, when seeing a red light, we will not need to interrupt our conscious mind by saying "excuse me, I need you (the conscious mind) to decide where to put my foot on? The brake? Or the accelerator?" Instead, our subconscious mind will bypass our conscious mind's notice or awareness and "automatically react" and hit the brake immediately without our conscious awareness and decision! With "auto-piloting" our deep conditionings will take us to the most familiar place they always go!

Theta brain–wave generates deep hypnotic state, leaving deep imprints on our emotive brain

Using the above example, imagine the kind of automatic responses and auto-piloting we have in all aspects of our life based on our childhood's zillions of conditionings in how we emotionally react, think and behave: the ramifications are enormous! The stem-cell biologist, researcher and medical instructor Dr. Bruce Lipton (2005) states that the influence of our early childhood conditionings have most prominent impacts for the rest of our life. He states that this is because before the age of 7, our brain operates with the theta brain wave which puts us in a deep hypnotic state. Whatever the emotive impressions, reactions or conditionings are before age 7, we down download in high speed and huge quantity. They go straight to our deep emotive and instinctive parts of our brain from which we generate repeated patterns for the rest of our life until some issues become unbearable to us.

Luckily, life is very kind and generous to us. It provides us infinite opportunities and a huge scope of free wills for us to unlearn for the needed healing and growing. The pioneer metaphysician Stuart Wilde (1946-2013) who taught personal development and human etheric life-field observed that one positive thought can easily dissolve thousands of negative ones. *Thus, the snowballs of our negative self-views accumulated over decades require only a fraction of such time to melt down.* With our mindful awareness, discipline and persistence in our daily routine, we can undo the sheep-mind conditionings to fulfil our real potentials.

Two Levels of Truths:

Man-made truths and Universal truths

There are two ways of looking at who we are: one from the cosmic perspective which is called the higher truths; the other one from the human perspective which is called the man-made truths (Tipping, 1997). In my observations, *the higher truths always guide and empower us back to our true divine essence, rendering us the true inner freedom to soar high; whereas man-made truths often limit and weaken our spirit, holding us back from fulfilling our true divine and infinite potentials.* Without remembering the higher truths of our true Divine Nature, Identity and Principles, it is so easy for us to be manipulated and exploited. *The higher truths are the antidotes to the vulnerability and inadequacy we so often battle with in life.*

To differentiate: man-made truths operate through our societal customs, laws, political system, hierarchical power structure, traditions and religions especially when they overly or covertly support and promote the wellbeing for a few elites and minorities only. Because of the skewed distribution of wellbeing to only the elites, man-made truths vary depending on who are in charge of the power. They thus change from generation to generation, system to system, culture to culture, time era to time era. Even within the same contemporary period, the definitions of such truths differ from location to location because of the different power involved. They can be cleverly packaged or disguised under the name of "norms", "values", "deeds of honour", and "trends or taboos".

Whilst most norms, traditions and deeds are man-made concepts, they are however, an essential part of our duality world. One cannot learn about freedom without limitation and responsibility. They go hand in hand. My point is not about questioning everything that is man-made; but to stay independent in our thinking. If we can observe our human systems as if we are some aliens visiting the earth planet for the first time, it becomes much easier to see how well the systems are serving us. When in doubts, a good change with high principles in place is not a bad idea.

For example, in the name of "virtue", "loyalty" and "honour", the ancient Japanese samurais from a few centuries ago were well known for having to commit suicide when they failed in a battlefield or were forced to serve a new war lord. Whilst such acts are unthinkable to our modern minds, with the deep conditionings to associate suicide with "virtues", and "honour" as defined by the Japanese hierarchical power then, it is hard to break such man-made distorted truths. Clearly, it served to benefit the wellbeing and sustain the power for the elites at the cost of the majority others' wellbeing. The obedience of citizens to such conditionings reinforces the elites' power, only for the elites to set up the rules to maintain its own power structure.

With the "one size fits all" "squares", "should", "have to", "oughts" and "societal formulas of success", we are encouraged and conditioned to put on many "masks" which push us further and further away from our authentic selves. Whilst "masks" are part of life, having too many masks on inevitably pull us away from living our authentic self which brings up the "alienation", "loneliness" and "void" in life. With the lack of self-fulfilment, purpose and meaning in life, it is no wonder that we see the ancient Chinese Taoists (the oldest hippies in the Chinese history) seek to live a simplistic life away from the stifling feudal society; the Flower Generation in the 60's and 70's liberated themselves to protest against the wars; and the Japanese youth formed a Shinjuku subculture of Manga (cartoon - figures) dress-up for rebellion to a rather perfectionistic, conformity-based society. With us not able to differentiate our true Divine Identity and Nature from our man-made society-demanded masks, many of us feel very lost and live in the lies and self-denial in our modern living. We seek escapes through addiction or indulgence with recreational drugs, alcohol, addictions to work, money, power, sex, status to numb the pain, only to deepen our emptiness and void which is a vicious cycle.

To restore our wellbeing, we have to question whether or not any so-called truths honour all individuals with equal respect for everyone's wellbeing involved. *Often, man-made truths bear no merits other than the fact they are programmed to us zillions of times through our moment-to-moment day in and day out reinforcements in all aspects of our life throughout our life span.* Such is exactly how "sheep mind" is formed and reinforced.

Higher truths on the other hand have been consistent for eons despite the variation of culture, time, location or situations. This applies to all species, all sentient beings in this universe, for example, all higher Cosmic Laws such as the Law of Physics, the Law of Balance, the Law of Manifestation and the Law of Cycle apply to all sentient beings the same and equally, regardless of their societal ranks, status, characteristics and circumstances. *The universal truths stand by themselves whether we understand, accept, validate them or not. With the universal truths, there are no squares, no criteria nor any exceptions to their ruling: they respects every living being the same without criteria or conditions.*

Man-Made Truths:

How man-made conditioning works

We have adapted our man-made truths or conditioning since day one when incarnating on this planet earth. Our human world has created lots of "squares" or "criteria" for us to fit in throughout our life span for thousands of years. *If we fit in or conform, we are included as "us", and treated as "normal", "special" and "superior". If not, we are excluded as the "outsiders", "outcasts"," abnormal", "deviates", and "inferior".*

The inferior status makes us vulnerable which reinforces us with the incentives to fit into more squares and norms to improve our worth (as conditioned). This is because when we are vulnerable, it is easier for us to be influenced and manipulated. Therefore, when being commanded to jump, we can say, "how high"? On the contrary, if we are empowered as equal and competent, when commanded so, we are more likely to say, "why should we?"

Man-made conditionings begin at our birth

If our real worth were $100, we are not deemed as $100 instantly in the human society upon our birth. Instead, our human world has created many "squares", "boxes" and "norms" for us to "fit in". *None of them are defined by us: ultimately, we get to "have no say" about our worth as individuals. We lose our innate power by giving away our say of our self-worth.*

The conditionings go like this: upon birth, if we are born fit, happy and healthy, we will earn our first $10 worth and will be treated as $10 worth because we "fit in" to the norm of "fit, happy and healthy". If however, we happen to have two heads but one body, the world news would broadcast about us because we "deviate" from the norm. The head-turnings, funny looks, judgements, gossips and discriminations we receive in our day in and day out events would make us feel like $9 worth only.

By the time we are twelve months old, most babies can manage to sit up, stand up, calling "mama" or "dada" with proper eye-contacts. If we fit into this category, we earn another ten dollars' self-worth for ourselves, making it $20 worth now. However, if all we can do is to roll around in a sick bed, not able to sit up nor stand up, make funny noises, drooling and rigid eye contacts; we are treated like $8 only. Despite having a few toddlers that play around with us to start out, many of them will be steered away by their parents behind the scene because we are deemed as "handicapped", "inferior" and "not one of us"!

By age four or five, most of us have to go to kindergarten or preschool. If we can "sit still and comply", and "prove" that we can read our "ABC" and count our "one, two, three", we are deemed as "intelligent". With "proof" that we are "intelligent", we fit in again. We are treated like $30. However, if we have some speech delays, learning difficulties such as ADD (Attention Deficit Disorder), ADHD (Attention Deficit Hyperactive Disorder), autism or some disabilities and deformity, we are deemed as "nuisance", "troubles", "stupid", "misfits", and "headaches". When other children refuse to sit next to us, play with us or call us names, and we are sent to the school principal's office for discipline or sent home earlier because of the "troubles" we create, we are deemed and treated like $7 only!

Unfortunately, everywhere we turn to for a different answer and treatment in our society, we get more of the same reactions mostly because the majority of us have been subject to the similar conditionings since birth. Despite the unjust treatments, when asking our parents why things are the way they are in our society, we often get the same answers that "that's just the way it is". After years of getting such answers, we eventually give up asking and accept that "that's just the way it is". The man-made norms have become our "comfort zones" after a while. *The constant and persistent reinforcements and comfort zones perpetuate even more of the same belief that we all have to "fit in" the "squares" as defined externally to earn our self worth!*

Whether these conditioned beliefs are functional or not, they all inevitably leave strong subconscious deep imprints on our minds. Years later, these *subconscious conditionings continue to affect our emotional, thinking and behavioural modes.* By the time we reach age 21, it is no wonder that we have long forgotten that we are truly powerful and magnificent divine entities with divine nature and infinite potential. Instead of beaming our true glow of 500, 000 watts, we beam 50 watts only! We have become the products of our man-made conditionings, replaying our self-doubt programming until we fit in, prove it, achieve it, earn it, impress others, please others, compromise and sacrifice us to justify our worth. We keep bending backward by giving away our power and yet, *the more we give, the more we have to give. It's a never-ending rat-race servicing no one but a handful of minorities until we awake to the Higher Universal Truths.*

The man-made formulas for human worth

As the result of human conditionings, our formulas of self-worth go like this:

- I am worthy only if I fit in.
- I am worthy only if my family are normal without dysfunction, drama or traumas.
- I am worthy only if my family are rich.
- I am worthy only if my body size is within normal range.
- I am worthy only if I am good looking, popular and smart.
- I am worthy only if I am successful, earning top incomes.
- I am worthy only if my significant others validate me so.
- The bigger the income I produce, the more worthy I am.
- The higher the social status I achieve, the more superior I am.
- The more influential, prestigious and famous I am, the more worthy I am.
- If only I can impress the whole world, I'd be able to justify why I am super worthy.

- If only my mother can love me as much as she loves my sister, I'd be worthy.
- If overnight I lost all of my earning and assets, I am just useless, a failure and nobody!

The list goes on and on....

Externally-defined truths makes us vulnerable and disempowered

With our worth being defined by others, by society, by traditions, by any authorities, our religious leaders, our parents, our spouse, our peers, our next door neighbours *or anyone else but ourselves, we literally have no power to our most precious self-worth no matter how much we achieve.* Just when we think we finally fit into the squares and meet with the bars, the whole set of bars and squares are changed beyond our control. It's therefore, a *never-ending rat-race.*

In addition, with our worth outside of our control, it also means that we are forever on *a roller-coaster ride*! When life treats us nicely, we feel like $2000 worth; when life treats us badly, we feel like $2 only. When others praise us and love us, we feel like $2,000,000 worth; when they abandon us and choose to move on with the other, we feel like $5 worth only!

This explains why despite having gorgeous body and images, earning millions and billions of dollars, owning luxury and having powerful influences and prestige, most of celebrities or movie stars still go through their cat fights, depression, drug rehabs and overdose. They have not been exempt from the rat race either. *With our self-worth being externally defined, we are forever living other people's versions and definitions of success, happiness, identity and fulfilment but not ours!* If our true innate capacity is to beam 500,000 watts (as emitted by our inner sacred jewels), by allowing others' definitions to rule our self-worth, we are dimming our light to 50 watts only.

By the time we die, we live a life impressing the whole world but ourselves. There is success and applause, but there is no self-fulfilment nor joy. No wonder not having the guts to put aside others' nay says to follow our inner callings is one of the top regrets at our death beds in Australia!

*Has it not dawned on us that "self"-worth should come from our "selves" to begin with? Ultimately, our self-worth has nothing to do with what we own, do or have, it's to do with **how** our self-worth is defined!* If it's externally-defined, we will be doomed with misery even if we achieve the highest high of all (because we still give away the power as if we don't know our true self-worth better). *If it's internally-defined, we finally will have our own say about our worth, and we can be self-content and self-appreciative irrespective of what the others define or say about us!*

Small Homework:

For the rest of our life, on the moment to moment basis, whenever we feel down and inadequate, not worthy enough, say and act deliberately with chin-up:

"I am worth100 no matter what!"

凡爾賽的
玫瑰之一
1996
1.6

Chapter iii

Remember Our Real Selves

"We are all made of the same materials
like the sun, the moon, and the stars.
What the sun, the moon,
the stars are capable of, we are."
— Anonymous

Outside the Square

One of my favourite stories in my childhood was <u>Jonathan Livingston Seagull</u> by Richard Bach. In a metaphoric way, the author gently reminds us that we have the unlimited power and creativity to be whatever we set ourselves to be. Whilst most other seagulls are busy fighting over their fish and territory, Jonathan Livingston Seagull wants to fly faster than the speed of sunlight. Despite being ridiculed by all other seagulls as a fool, after years of trial and error, passion, faith and persistence, he has mastered it and become the inspiration for generations of seagulls to come. Sometimes, life's answers and profound truths are to be read in between lines beyond the squares; beyond the logics, tradition, "should" and **"have to"** beyond the limitations of our five senses.

Currently, we are on the edge of completing a huge cycle. According to the Mayan Calendar, not only have we just completed a 26,000 years' great cycle, we have also completed a 104,000 years' cosmic cycle with planetary movement entering into a brand new phase astrologically and astronomically. The implication is that we are entering "the photon band and the Aquarius Age", receiving an enormous amount of light from the sun (Barbara Hand Clow, 1995). According to Hand Clow, this intense light from the photon band is the catalyst to awaken our deep knowing of who we are as multi-dimensional light beings. We are at the most potent edge of making a quantum leap for our human evolution into a much higher dimension, to reclaim our bountiful divine heritage. Many of us are awakening to our divine essence as the children of the Great Creator. *Literally, we are all gods and goddess within us!*

Higher Truths

As mentioned earlier, great saints and philosophers and sages often derive their truths based on observing the nature and cosmos surrounding us. We need not go to the church nor any theology class to learn about who we are because the universal truths are in front of our very eyes and inside us. When we quiet our mind, and look up to the sky, to see and feel our position and role in this Universe: *like father, like son; as the children of our Great Creator, we are also mighty creators of our very own life.*

The following major Universal Truths help to remember our true identity and our divine worth.

We Are Innately Equal

The universe's most powerful forces that nurture and support hundreds of millions of species on earth are the four elements: the fire, earth, water and air. Despite our memory amnesia about our divine Soul Self, we are surrounded by the Universal Truths each moment of our life to remind us of our divinity.

When we observe nature, it is not difficult to see that the most powerful four elements that nurture all never discriminate, judge, criticise nor belittle any species or any living beings. The sun shines upon the mountain lion and the dung beetle the same. The rain showers upon the villain and the victim the same. The fresh air is made available to the butterfly and the moss the same. The soil offers its nurturance to a huge boulder and a tiny blade of grass the same. No criteria are required for these equal treatments to take place.

Ultimately, we are all different, unique and special, but deemed and treated as equal by the powerful four elements and our Great Universe! *Superiority and inferiority are invented concepts by the human world; they are not applicable in the domain of the Higher Truths.*

Once $100, forever $100!

Using the same metaphor from the last chapter, if our true worth is $100, despite having different batch numbers, each hundred dollars is no more, and no less than any other hundred dollars.

If the $100 note encounters some idiot that tears it apart, trashes it, and treats it like dirt and rubbish; despite the damages, when any onlooker picks it up, the onlooker is likely to respond, "what kind of bloody idiot would do something like this to this hundred dollars!", rather than "oh, this is now only $2", unless the onlooker does not have any common sense.

Without being emotionally attached, it is easy for any onlookers to see two things clearly. *First of all, the dollar value remains the same regardless of what has happened to it. Secondly, the terrible acts of wrong deeds done to the $100 reflects the "doer", "the offender", not the receiver (the $100 note).*

The biggest mistake we often make in life is that we tend to *take things too personally* with overly-simplified logic that "good things happen to good people, bad things happen to bad people; if bad things happen to me, it must be because I am not good enough!" Without realising that our innate divine worth cannot be altered nor redefined no *matter what*, many of us have continued to shortchange ourselves $98 worth for the rest of our life as a major mistake!

One might wonder why this poor act of severe damage and abuse happens to us only. The truth is: *the poor treatments happen to us not because we are unworthy, but because we believe that we are unworthy.* There is a major difference here! *This is because whatever we believe deep down inside, our Universe will prove us right.*

On the other hand, if the $100 note is well-cherished by someone who actually paints nice rainbows, glues some jingling bells, and does beautiful embroidery of flowers and butterflies and sprays perfume all over it to glorify it; despite the "specialness" of it, when we go to the bank and ask to exchange it for $5,000, we will still get $100 of equal value in return!

My point is: *"once a hundred, forever a hundred!"* No humiliating treatments nor circumstances can possibly devalue our true original divine equal worth. No special kingly, queenly treatments can possibly inflate our worth either. It is often said that for however magnificent and almighty our angels, archangels and ascending masters are, they always deem us the humans (gods and goddess within) as their equals like their brothers and sisters because we are truly all equally divine.

We Are Innately Perfect

Human world see "perfection" as a goal, a status or a destination. Often, it is equated with having a good upbringing, daunting parents, going to prestigious schools, securing a high income job, matching with some good-looking and successful spouse, producing high-achieving children, having many mansions, able to enjoy comfort and luxury in life and retire "happily ever after" without any trauma and dramas. Whilst this is one valid version of "perfection", *our Spirit world accommodates all sorts of creative and diverse versions of "perfection".*

From the spiritual perspective, "perfection" is not a goal; it is a journey. It's a forever-evolving and forever-expanding journey that entails all the elements of Yin and Yang, good and bad, high and low, bright and dark, easy and difficult, joyous and miserable, blissful or horrendous elements altogether as one.

Tough times and crisis are part of Perfection

Every day of our life, everyone that we encounter, everything that has happened to us are *parts of our journey of becoming perfect*. Perfection thus entails good times and bad times; the highs and the lows of our life. During the storm of crisis, as we demonstrate signs of not coping, our human world is quick to label us as "weak", "stupid", "mistake", "failure", "not good enough", "deserving it", "embarrassment", "being punished", or "having a bad karma". As the result of repeated conditionings, we are quick to harshly judge ourselves too, thus the famous saying, "we are our worst enemies". However, our

Great Universe has none of such language of judgements and put-downs. When a new born puppy has difficulty standing up like all his other puppy siblings, we don't see any mother dogs growling with put-downs to shame and label the puppy, but gently and lovingly licking and nurturing him until he can stand up properly to blend in with all other puppies. We see many species doing the same. Some mother dogs even nurture orphaned kittens without discrimination or exclusion.

Vulnerability and mistakes are normal parts of many learning curves we all go through in life

In our human societies, we are treated as if beyond the teenage years, we suddenly have become perfect, flawless, and impeccable at all times miraculously simply because we are adults! The reality cannot be any more opposite! Vulnerability, mistake, difficulty, trials and errors are the inevitable and thus, normal parts of many learning curves we the entire humanity all go through inevitably in life. Throughout human history, there has not been one human that has never made any mistakes nor never felt vulnerable! Not even the kings, queens or saints can be exempt from such; what makes us think that we can be any different? If so, then, why such a harsh self-criticism and self-judgement?

Everything takes time and practice before we make things better towards near-perfection. In <u>Conversations with God</u>, the author, Neale Donald Walsch conveyed God's message that "progress" is a far better goal to aim at than "perfection" because "absolute perfection" in the duality world does not exist: all is individually defined and is subject to relativity. To aim at "progressing" is a better way of approaching life since the "perfection is a forever evolving, and forever expanding journey" (Walsch, 1995). Just when we think we are perfect, someone has come up with something even better. Being able to be content with our own progress rather than having to be perfect is a much more gracious way of approaching life.

Crises are "boot-camps" in our life to accelerate our learning

In nature, when a plant is challenged by a drought, even though it might wilt temporarily, to survive, the plant will search far and near to access its needed water and nutrients. At the end of the 6 months' drought, instead of remaining 1 metre within its origin, the root has stretched to 15 metres radius from its origin, way outside of its comfort zone, hardy and well-established. By the same token, when pruned, a tree can grow much bigger in volume in a short time in comparison to those that are not pruned. Who says the hardship in life is not part of the perfection? Instead of seeing hardship and vulnerability as "punishment" and "victimhood", from the bigger point of view, it is more a "boot-camp" designed as a condensed training to accelerate our learning and growth in life. The boot-camp empowers us for "master hood", therefore, instead of asking "why me", we say, "Thank you for the divine training for perfection!" It may not be easy to do; but it's a better way to go about it. Making peace with the hardship allows us to rise above the situation by leaving the negatively conditioned emotions behind whilst getting onto the tasks of growing smoother.

We Are Innately Complete

Completeness means that by us being us, there is no need to justify, prove, conform, acquire, achieve, fit in or compromise, please, impress or sacrifice ourselves in order to earn our worthiness. In the human world, we are taught many "only ifs" that puts conditions and limitations to our worth. However, our Great Universe is complete and powerful in its own existence; it requires no conditions from us before rendering our divine worth. The "should" and "have-to" are often requirements invented by our human system. They are mostly designed for easy mass manipulation to suit a few elites' needs. It may or may not have anything to do with the Higher Truths.

Wouldn't it be nice that instead of "should" and "have to", that we do things because we "want to" and "choose to" or "are inspired to" and "aspire to"?

My point again is not to negate the validity of being responsible in our society entirely, but to *challenge with the question*: "*to what degree do we allow ourselves to go by these conditioned obligations blindly especially when it is against our inner truths and when it is at the cost of our very wellbeing?*" Responsibility has its roles in maintaining the stability and freedom in human growth and development. My point is in not "over-using" it to such a degree that it brings up self-denial, self-belittlement and self-alienation which prevent us from being self-fulfilled and expressing our true divine nature and potential.

When we turn within, all is complete

Many people remark, "If only my mother can love me the way she loves my sister, my life will be complete." I say to them, "If only we can love ourselves the way we want to be loved by anyone, our lives will be complete." There is a Taiwanese proverb that says, "when leaning upon a mountain, the mountain will crumble one day.

When leaning upon a person, the person will age one day. When leaning upon ourselves, nothing beats it!"

We are Eternal and Infinite

Being multi-dimensional energy beings means that upon death, we shed our physical body and our soul essence passes on to where we come from to the higher dimension. Many of our deceased loved ones choose to be our guides in their energy form. They continue to love and support us in most aspects of our life. Our relationships continue to develop despite their passing over. They often bring us messages of love, hope and forgiveness and foresights for us to move on in peace throughout our life's remaining journey (Martin and Romanowski, 2003).

We are made of love and light. Love and light never die. We simply change from one form to another, carrying our spiritual body and essence as we move across dimensions. We come in empty-handed, we go home empty-handed. What we go home with is the experience, the actual tastes of life whatever version or definition we choose to explore. There is no death nor real separation. Deaths are but beginning of reunion with our deceased beloved ones in the "after life" on the other side. Nothing is lost. All is here if only we see it from a much bigger perspective beyond this physical plane.

Small Homework

Take as many small but different actions as possible throughout the whole day, switch on your mindfulness, and deliberately

Love,	*Appreciate,*	*Support,*
Cherish,	*Acknowledge,*	*Forgive,*
Accept,	*Believe in,*	*Honour,*
Approve of,	*Stand by,*	

Nurture your Inner Child, as if you are his or her best parent or best mate ever!

Other acts to foster self love is to use the language of love, kindness, patience, encouragement, and comfort to ourselves in moments of defeats and say to ourselves:

"I love you and adore you just the way you are."

"I don't care about the whole world, I am here with you and for you."

"I believe in you and stand by you!"

"I know you can do it."

"One small step at a time. No need for a big stress now."

"The only meaningful comparison is between my Now and my Past."

"With or without success, with or without progress, the fact that you have tried and are willing to step outside your comfort zone, I am proud of you already!"

"月下老人的忠告"
嬲璞於黄金海岸 1993年 5月6日

Chapter iv
Decoding Life's Mystery: Why Me?

"You've come back into the Realm of the Physical over and over again in order to embrace the fullness of this experience, because you seek to understand all of it, thoroughly and completely.

.... You have been all of it in your lifetimes. The victim and the villain, the strong and the weak, the oppressed and the oppressor, the so-called 'right', and the so-called 'wrong', so so-called 'good' one and the so-called 'bad' one."
— *God, as speaking through Neale Walsch (2017)*

Many of us who have lived through life's major challenges and hardships often wonder "why me?" with a "poor me" reaction. We are often puzzled if there is a God or Higher Intelligence, then how come there is so much injustice, cruelty and tragedy in life; and why others are not given the same difficult situations to tolerate and endure like us? To solve this life's puzzle, it requires that we go beyond our usual linear thinking and see life from a much bigger perspective.

We are on the same boat

We are on the same boat called "humanity". If the others around us are not having the same lesson, chances are that they have chosen very different lessons at this time. Just because we love English and poetry, it does not mean that everyone else is or will be taking the same. Even when others are taking the same courses, they might be on a more advanced level or a lower level than us depending on whether they have entered the learning earlier or, learnt a bit faster or slower than us..

Even though we take the same courses and lessons, the way we learn varies from individual to individual, teacher to teacher, time era to time era, culture to culture, galaxy to galaxy. All is unique. There is no right or wrong way of learning; there are only easier or harder ways of learning. Some take longer routes with lots of side-tracks and self-defeats; others are focused like laser-beams and get there faster. Whichever way we learn, we all eventually graduate from the life's courses to exit the Cosmic Wheel.

No one is ever alone: we evolve as a team together

No one is ever alone, including the orphans. Our true origin is this Great Universe. Our biological parents are the physical vehicles that we have pre-chosen to enter into this physical reality. With or without their physical presence in our lives, look up to the stars and we know where we belong.

No one exists in a vacuum. Our learning journey is composed of visible friends, family, workmates, spouses, in-laws, associates, seemingly random strangers, accidental events and circumstances and the invisible team of our guidance, angels, master teachers etc. from the other side. Many people observe that most of their major milestone decisions and learnings occur in the context of "coincidences" and "synchronicity".

Our invisible team plays a crucial part of our spiritual evolvement

These seeming coincidences and amazing synchronicity are the evidence of our invisible team of support at work from the other side! Even when it looks like we are very "alone" and feel "lonely", it is often because we believe that the visible world is all there is. We have either shut out our spirit world's team of soulmates, guides and friends we have known life time after life time in our darkest moments, or that we simply discount them as merely our imagination or meaningless dream figures.

Since birth, each one of us is escorted by at least two invisible angel-guidance who have mastered their lessons and accepted to be our spiritual guides before our birth throughout our life's journey to the moment we die (Coll, 1995). We have prechosen them to be our guides for our spiritual advancement whilst taking on this physical journey here. They give us insights, intuition, direct knowing via gentle nudges, whisper, glimpses of future, goose bumps and flashes of images or thoughts to put us on the easier tracks. They love, nurture, support and guide us but never interfere with our free wills until we "ask". They will only intervene without our asking when there is a death threat when we are not meant to die yet. Also, depending on the level of our advancement, as our life unfolds into different stages, we are assigned with different and extra guides and teachers. How could we possibly ever be alone?

The grass is not always greener on the other side

When we struggle in life, we tend to take things personally and put ourselves down as conditioned in the human system. As we criticise and judge ourselves as not good enough and unworthy, we inevitably and relatively also over-idealise others at the same time. Coming from a low down position of poor self-esteem, everything we project from that self-defeating position is "distorted" with "over- exaggeration" in a way that is completely out of proportion. And often times, we do so without realising so.

No one's life is all-perfect as we project. Yes, they appear very happy and fulfilled upfront at work, but at home, they might have a teenage son who is addicted to drugs with run-aways and legal offenses that break their hearts. Yes, your next door neighbour's wife may look drop-dead gorgeous upfront but the reality is she battles with eating disorder, and as a couple, they fight like cats and dogs behind the scene beyond our knowing. Yes, your childhood classmates may look like they earn millions and billions and travel around the world, and they are able to give tons of money to their never-working adult children, but they are traumatised as one of the children has a marriage break down whilst the other has a life-threatening illness. Stories like this can go on and on.

Until we get to know the person in depth, we don't know their stories. We truly don't know where they have come from, what they are facing, and where they are heading... *Judging from the surface, especially when we feel belittled and inadequate ourselves, could create the illusion of "why me only?" and "poor me" as if we are alone. In reality, we all have challenges and lessons to learn one way or the other; no one is an exception.* This is what I meant by being in the same boat, and that the grass is not always greener on the other side.

When the lessons are easier, it does not make any one of us luckier, better or superior than the others. It simply means that in the huge spectrum of time, we are moving along in our individuations in our own unique pace and timing. Sooner or later we all have to face similar humanity lessons in different time and space and circumstances one way or the other. Focalising our existence in one life time gives us no clue but rather distorted views that some are favoured by the Universe with huge blessings or fortunes whilst others are not. *However, when we stretch our views across dimensions and different life times, we will quickly realise how much similarity of lessons we all have to undertake before we ascend to higher dimensions.* Literally we are a bunch of travellers moving along the same direction towards one same destination which is our Origin, Love, and God.

Life is Purposeful and Meaningful

> *"I asked for Courage… and*
> *God gave me danger and fears to challenge.*
> *I asked for Love… and*
> *God gave me troubled people to help.*
> *I asked for strength… and*
> *God gave me obstacles to overcome.*
> *At the end, I got nothing I wanted;*
> *I got everything I needed."*
> *— Source unknown*

One may ask what about those whose children died young, people that are tormented by tragedy and traumas and significant loss, illness or disability. When we look beyond these events and tragic circumstances, despite the surface look of injustice, seeming punishment and suffering that appear to make no sense, the journeys and circumstances do offer potent grounds for us to stretch our wings, our creativity, use our courage, test our wisdom, cultivate our dormant tenacity, patience, and ability to love, move mountains, forgive and share.

Precisely because we are paired up with a disabled sibling, we learn to love and genuinely care for those that are less fortunate with nonjudgemental compassion in a much more profound way. The former American President, John Kennedy, had a sister who was handicapped with inability for basic self-care all her life. Her daily struggle and conditions had triggered the deep empathy and compassion in Kennedy. When Kennedy became a member of the US Congress, he was the first to pass a civil bill to ensure that tons of other families having similar challenges were looked after financially and medically with community and government support. Life's perfection works in mysterious way: within imperfection, there is perfection. Who says a person with disability cannot contribute to humanity?

Precisely because we come from dirt broke family upbringing, we are prone to become fiercely independent, capable and mature from a much younger age. This paves the ground for one's outstanding achievements later. The former American president Lincoln is one good example of this. Precisely because we are deaf, mute or blind, we now have to stretch our creativity, imagination whilst using every bit of our tenacity, patience, intelligence and faith to get the basics to work. Helen Keller's life story is an excellent example of such. We may not be Kennedy, Lincoln or Helen Keller but we all have our equally divine and magnificent sacred jewel-like potentials in us for us to activate.

We are our life's writer, actor, director and editor

Literally, we write our own life scripts before our birth as guided by our master guides who work with us incarnation after incarnation. We are also the editor, actor and director of our life. The Great Universe and our angelic teams are our co-creators, mirroring back and orchestrating for us constantly what we create from within us. The hurdles and journey are pre-chosen which is the "fate" aspect of our life; but it is our free wills that determine the outcomes which we call "destiny".

Our Attitude Determines the Outcome

When the Universe drops one big stone in front of us, it does not come with a command that we have to treat it as a "blocking stone". Despite the common human conditioning to see any stones as "blocking stones", we can relearn to approach them as the "stepping stones". After all, what does not kill us, makes us stronger.

Boot-camps are deliberately designed for condense learning

Trees that are pruned often grow faster and stronger. Iron that undergoes hammering in the 1000 degree fire turns into steel: it is more durable than ever. Greenhouse offers nice and comforting environment for a tree but it also limits its true potential. Humans on the physical realm operate similarly. Many famous movie stars come from very tough upbringings which pre-expose them to a huge variety of challenges. By the time they are adults, they stand out because of the "condensed boot- camp trainings" they have received earlier from their life's experiences. Marlon Brando from "the Godfather",

Gerard Depardieu from "Jean de Florette", and Zhou, Ren Fa from "Crouching Tiger, Hidden Dragon" are excellent examples of such. Their ongoing exposures to diverse and tough experiences in their youth have wellprepared them to instinctively know about humanity first-hand thus paving the good foundation to their exceptional good acting on the big silver screen years later. Similarly, by the time we die, hopefully, we have the pride and honour to say, "precisely because of our life's journeys, we have evolved brilliantly!"

The level of hardship is the barometer to our strength

From the spiritual perspective, it is an honour when we are "granted" permission to take on our condense course in a "bootcamp" in life. This is because prior to our birth on the Spirit Realm, not all pre-chosen life lessons are granted automatically. There is no comparison between climbing a Himalayan mountain in Tibet and climbing the Blue Mountains in Australia.

In order for our pre-chosen lessons to be granted, our master guides along with the Elders (the very Wise, Loving, Old Ones) would look into our "Akashic records" which contain our soul's past, present and future, to decide whether we are mature and strong enough to take on such a journey. If not, some delays and alterations will be made to better suit the soul's level of evolvement.

It is truly an honour when we are given very crappy stuff in life to overcome, because our angelic team support and Higher Soul know how "ready" and "mature" and "capable" we are. However, because of our human conditionings to gravitate towards only comfort, pleasure and glamour, once incarnated on earth, we tend to see these hurdles as "punishment" and "misfortune". Seeing life from a much bigger timeline across dimensions and lifetimes, we can make peace with the challenges by facing them sincerely: the very irritation we get in life is the very essence we use to create the pearl of life.

Misfortunes are blessings in disguise

To learn about self-acceptance and self-love, we may take on the extreme challenge of being gay. Our harsh human discriminations against the gay identity will serve to test our own self-loyalty and self-strength to see if we have the guts to declare and be who we truly are, despite the whole world's protest against our identity.

Whilst a child's death may evoke years of guilt and depression, on the deeper level, it also stimulates the survived parents' ability to cherish and appreciate every moment in life as it comes. It also prompts the quench to search for deeper purpose and meaning of life which will inevitably accelerate their spiritual development. Such are the unique gifts brought upon by the departed souls which continue to exist on the other side eternally. On the other hand, deceased children may be "advanced souls" who need not go through another lengthy lifetime of incarnation. They simply chose to come in for a short time for the sake of accelerating their parents' spiritual growth. Overall, whatever the "big picture" is, we simply have to trust our journey here is ultimately for our highest good and for the highest good of all, regardless the surface seeming tragedy.

One Final Note

With the content in this Chapter, please do not mistake me as saying that we cannot grow or evolve in nice, easy and happy ways. The truth is we do learn and grow either way. What I believe is that if it's an awesome ride, be content, appreciative and celebrate it. But when it is not, let's understand it's not because we are bad, stupid, unworthy or deserve any punishment. *Let's make peace with it and get on with it without victimhood or blame but the understanding that there is a big picture and good reason for all this to happen.* There is a famous Taiwanese saying: "In crisis, heroes are created; in heroes, histories are made." Ultimately, we are all our heroes in our own life. Easy or hard, there is no victim involved. In <u>Emerging out of Cocoon</u>, the Taiwanese author Hsieh, Ming-Jieh (2015) states that in conversations with his Inner God, his Inner God says he "sends only the angels and the teachers" to us. The former make us glow; the latter make us grow. Literally, we have no enemies in life.

Small Homework

For this week, take 5 to 10 minutes to reflect on the goods and the bads each day. With the good things that happen to you or around you, be very thankful with deep appreciation. Go out to celebrate all joys you have and share them with everyone around you to amplify the good.

With the things that make you feel bad, greet them with openness, also with gratitude that they are here to make us grow.

To greet, affirm:

"Everything happens for a good reason in the bigger picture of life."

"Every hardship is designed for me to activate my hidden jewels within."

"There is always rainbow at the end of a storm."

"There is no coincidence in life."

"There are no victims in life; our perceptions make it so."

"Bad things do not last forever; the best is yet to come."

"All journeys good or bad, high or low are part of the Ultimate Perfection."

"The level of my hardship is the barometer to my soul's strength."

"The higher the mountain I am given to climb, the more capable and courageous I am deemed by the Great Universe."

Approach the challenge without self-judgement. If you need further support, do seek professional help immediately.

Chapter v
Travel Lightly: Externalisation

"If you want to fly, give up everything that weighs you down."
— *the Original Buddha*

In human relationships, it is not uncommon that "shit happens". When shit happens, as conditioned by our human system, we tend to judge ourselves based on the final end results, regardless of the efforts and good intents we invest in the journey. As the unjust occurs, we often fail to differentiate our deeds from those of others. Worse yet, we would carry this unjust rubbish on our shoulders and blame ourselves blindly continuously.

To travel lightly in life, it requires that we unload the rubbish that is not ours and get onto fulfilling our inner jewels. I have observed that many of us confuse rubbish with jewels in life. This is how we make our life unnecessarily stinky, heavy and miserable. By "rubbish", I refer to others' unfair abandonment, rejection, abuse, discrimination, accusation, sabotage, judgements, and criticism of us. By "rubbish", I also refer to life's injustice, tragedies, loss, grief and dramas that happen to us beyond our control, beyond our fair shares without any wrongdoing on our ends.

When these unfortunate events occur to us in our youth, we tend to take these events very personally, as if the whole world "revolves around us", as if everything "happens because of us". Such tendency is what I call "Internalisation". Without confronting such Internalisation tendency, unfortunately, as adults, many of us continue to "internalise" others' issues and responsibility as a persistent pattern. We continue the self-blame with "what's wrong with me?" instead of asking also "what's wrong with the others, and the system!"

Origin of internalisation

The Internalisations are often sabotaged and reinforced by a dysfunctional environment, be it our upbringing, schooling, or any unhealthy societal systems. As mentioned earlier, any "differences" in the human world are deemed as "inferior" and tend to cast us as the "outsiders". It could be that our parents are drug-addicts and they are hugely irresponsible, leaving us physically and emotionally neglected to struggle without the basics. It could be that our family are targets of gossips and scandals because the narrow-minded community we live in does not tolerate our religious or racial differences. It can be that we are "the Little Ugly Duckling" or "the Black Sheep" within the family because being the Light Workers or the Star Seeds, we don't fit into our family's extreme materialistic way of defining life. It can be that our humanitarian thoughts are too advanced for our human corruptive system a century ahead of its time, thus we struggle all our life without proper rewards or recognition. How our government systems favoured Thomas Edison's models of money-making over Nicola Tesla's for clean and free energy supply is a good example of such.

The way out

Internalisation is a dysfunctional way of relating to others. It is not to be confused with the concepts of self-reflection and self-responsibility because the former has the "unfair" elements involved where we hold ourselves overly-responsible for others' problems without a healthy boundary to deflect. *Internalisation means we "blindly" and "automatically assume" it's our fault, "without proper differentiation" of whose responsibility it is, and jump straight to question, doubt and criticise ourselves unfairly and entirely*

Simply put, when we internalise issues that are not ours, we do ourselves "injustice". It's much like sentencing ourselves for others' crimes. We judge ourselves unfairly because our selfboundary is weakened with tendency to rely on external feedbacks as conditioned and reinforced often by our human society. We blame ourselves fully when in higher truth, the sabotage can come from the others' biased projection onto us, because of their past unresolved trauma; verbal put-downs and wicked intents towards us, due to their own jealousy and insecurity; aggression and mistreatments to us due to their terrible personalities and free wills to manipulate.

With Internalisation, we are confused with where others' responsibility ends and where ours begins. It hinders us with low self-worth, repeated relationship difficulties, victimhood, and over-compromisation whilst being treated as doormats in life. However, not even our judicial system would hold anyone responsible for another person's deeds! Interestingly, when we pass over to the other side, it's ultimately our deeds not the others' deeds that Higher self will be reviewing for our soul's evolvement. Therefore, likewise, whilst being alive on earth planet, if we can satisfy our Higher Conscience when evaluating our own deeds, that should be good enough. To resolve, "Externalisation" is the antidote to bring back our good senses and restore our wellbeing.

Externalisation with Two -Sided Mirror

Whenever we encounter unfair situations in life, it is very important that we use Externalisation as a defence and emotional immune system to protect our wellbeing. There are three steps for Externalisation: to self-reflect, differentiate and deflect.

Step 1: Self –Reflect with our Higher Conscience

My deeds reflect me and are my responsibility

Our deeds are composed of our deliberate thoughts, speech, intent and conduct throughout our life span. When we encounter something unfair, step one is to self-reflect by asking ourselves, *"Have I deliberately thought of something bad; spoken of unkind words; intended something malicious; or acted in a very harmful way that I have caused this poor reception?"*. If the answer is honestly "yes" as judged by our own Higher Conscience, then we fully claim our responsibility and ownership of the deed(s). We do something to problem-solve to improve the situation or prevent the same from happening again.

If the answer is no, then the energy that undermines our deeds on the giving ends does *not* come from us; we then go to Steps 2 and 3.

 If after doing our best to fix the problems through and through, and the reception is still not achieved (because the others refuse to forgive or continue to project their issues onto us for whatever the reasons), then *we can make peace with ourselves whilst staying detached from the end results* to *remain emotionally independent.* This is because *we simply have no control over others' reactions and free wills towards our efforts, but at least we can say, we honestly have done the best we can in that situation without regrets.*

Step 2: Differentiate others' deeds

In step two, we place a two-sided mirror in the middle of the relationship between us and the others, and say, "What I think, what I speak, what I intend and how I act reflect me." However, *"What the others think of me, speak of me, intend towards me, and act towards me reflect them, not me!"* This is because despite us being the targets, the very subject (the owner and doer) of these acts are "the others", not us. However intelligent or stupid these thoughts are projected onto us; however truthful or defaming the spoken words are said about us; however regal or malicious the intents are aimed towards us; however kind or damaging the acts are done to us, the "doers" are "the others". These deeds reflect their free wills, unless we have a gun aiming at them to manipulate their free wills. *How the others respond to us is thus what the angels call "none of our business" zone.*

Our erroneous self-blame is a conditioned response

Our society often conditions us to judge ourselves based on the end results which is unfair because "we can only lead the horse to the water, but cannot make it drink". *By doing all the right things, if the horse does not appreciate our effort of leading it to the water, but kicks our butt and runs away, it does not mean that we are lousy or not good enough; it simply means that there is a mismatch*! Whilst we are conditioned by our family or society to rely on the horse or the onlookers to give us the feedback on how good we are, what if it's a wild horse or a dumb one? What if the onlookers are not as switched-on with their judgement? We will be wasting our time to wait for any fair feedback from such situations. Instead, we bring our power back to be emotionally and spiritually independent by saying "by me doing the best I can at the time, I deem myself as good enough"!

Step 3: Cancel, Delete, Clear to deflect and disown others' deeds

Imagine each one of us operates like a nation of its own. Our custom is our immune and defence mechanism and our Higher Conscience is our Customs Officer. Just because anyone arrives at our doorway at the border does not mean that we automatically have to open our custom to let them in. Our Customs Officer reserves the right to decide what suits to come into our territory. Here, our Customs Officer is not our egos which are usually fear, lack and materialistically-based; but our Higher Conscience which operates with love, oneness, with wise discernment and is a far better judge. If someone says "blabla, blabla, bla... ", and our Higher Conscience deems it as truthful and suitable to our wellbeing, we can open our door to welcome it. *If not, we Cancel, Delete, and Clear to deflect and disown from our territory (or energy field). We can visualise it being thrown into a big flame of fire. Or we flush that low-vibe energy down the toilet where it belongs. Doing so allows us to be fair with ourselves whilst reserving our self-authority and respect.* When in doubt, simply treat the unjust in life as if "stepping upon a pile of dog-poohs". With dog-poohs, we simply wash them off and brush the bad vibes away without talking or dwelling on them further. It's just not worth it!

By disowning others' unjust deeds towards us, we are recognising that *irrespective of our benevolent deeds on the giving ends, others' deeds towards us depend on their upbringing, values, personalities, maturity, perspectives, choice and free wills which are their responsibility, unless we do something to manipulate and threaten their free wills.*

The bait is powerful only if we bite it.

Likewise, if others toss out a big bait towards us, knowing that there is an ugly hook underneath it and we still choose to bite it, it is our fault. This is because even though we are on the receiving end, it still takes two to "tango". *Just because others toss out a bait, we still have the free will to ignore it and walk away from their manipulation. Better yet, we can redefine the game by saying, "I will co-participate in this situation only if you show some decency, honesty and respect to me. Otherwise, I am out of here,"*

Many people I encounter live with the wounds of being treated like doormats after bending backwards to give endlessly to their beloved ones. Unbeknown to them, by bending backwards and allowing themselves to be treated like doormats, the act itself shows no self-respect already. With low self-respect, it emits low vibrational frequency. With such low frequency, it attracts like-energy of low vibes of disrespect from others. Many do heal the relationship once they walk away from such a harmful vicious cycle.

By embracing their sacred inner jewels with Externalisation over time, many do attract others' love and respect that match with their new self-love and respect as a transformation from inside out. Such is what I meant by "travel lightly" in life.

Love heals and transcends all

Whilst Externalisation helps us to restore our healthy boundary, and bring back our own power and dignity, it does not necessarily free us from attracting more of the same things as a pattern. This is particularly so when our mistrust towards others and life has not been healed. Over the years, in addition to working from within to improve the conditions, I have observed that another way of transcending any vicious cycle of "an eye for an eye" is to send prayers that express genuine blessing, forgiveness and gratitude for all involved. This coincides with the Ancient Hawaiian Shamanistic healing method called "Ho'oponopono".

As we take on this physical journey as spiritual energy beings, throughout eons of time, we have taken many different roles across the spectrum. Not all of our roles are of good characters. Most of our memories of our past existence were wiped out for the sake of staying focused on this current one at hand. In the big picture, we truly know not whether the injustice we receive is the cause or the effect without taking our past existence into consideration. The Hawaiian "Ho'oponopono" healing prayers literally covers a wide angle of life to heal all that are involved. It teaches us to say prayers as below:

" Dear ____,

I know not what brings upon this seeming unjust to me. If it's caused by my wrong deeds done to you in the past known or unknown to me, I sincerely ask for your forgiveness. If it's you who has wronged me, I forgive you and I forgive me. I bring back my power and stand firm in my power. I thank you for the lesson. I now release you with love. This is so, and so be it."

An eye for an eye is a common practice in human society because our ego is involved. Ego-based approach to counter-act often provokes further counter-reacts, which leads to further complications without ends. In many past life regression sessions, we often hear stories of enemies in the battlefields being paired up time and time again across different incarnations to work through their issues as a family, siblings, or couples, to learn to love for dissolving their karmic bonds.

"Karma" means life's learning. It is a neutral concept without the connotation of "sin" or "punishment". With life courses we flunk, we simply have to relearn until we pass all before graduating from our Cosmic Wheel. All in all, love and forgiveness offer fast-lane for evolvement because they make us rise above low vibes quickly. In Taiwan, there is a proverb that says, *"By yielding, our heart space opens up like the vast ocean and frees up like the infinite sky!"* Also, *"a family in harmony attracts abundance from all directions; a family in wars creates hardship without ends"*. The choice is ours.

What if it's hard to send love?

If it is hard for us to send love to our enemies or opponents, it is because we have not recognised the reason why the others attack us. It does not matter how the surface appears, the common underlying reason as to why the others attack us is because *they attack themselves the same way internally*! They have long forgotten who they truly are as sacred jewel-like beings because of our human societal conditionings. So much so that they *no longer remember their divine identity and what our true nature (which is love) feels like*!

If we understand that behind the façade, the attackers do not know better how to love themselves, and how they treat us is but a reflection of their internal world of no-love, emptiness and the lack; it would be easier for us to have the empathy and non-judgemental compassion for them. It would be easier for us to send them love and happiness. It's not always easy, but where there is a will, there is a way. With deliberate efforts and persistence, it can be done. I have seen many beautiful miracles of such human relationship transformations over the years because of love.

Small Homework:

When encountering unfair circumstances in life,

Step 1. To Self-Reflect, affirm:

- *I am willing to acknowledge and be responsible for my deeds.*
- *I am willing to problem- solve so that the same negative things do not repeat.*

Step 2. To differentiate, affirm:

- *I am willing to do my best in leading the horse to the water, but stay detached from the final end results.*
- *My happiness and worth no longer depend on the horse for validation; they depend on me recognising such in me independently. Using my Higher Conscience, if I deem my intent and effort as good enough, it is so, and so be it.*
- *Without wrongdoing, what I receive from the others reflects who they are. It is none of my business!*
- *When I make others' business my business, I am sentencing myself for the others' crimes.*

Step 3. To deflect, affirm the following:

- *Just because others say so does not automatically make it so.*
- *Just because others toss out a bait at me, I do not have to bite.*
- *At the face of an ugly bait, I have the choice to recognise the bait, ignore it, and act the opposite with cool, calm, collectedness.*

- *Better yet, I can transcend all these low down vibration by sending love and forgiveness to dissolve it all.*
- *When I send love, I become love myself. My opponents become love too. Love transcends all!*

Love Intelligently:
No More Over-Rescuing

Rescuers put everyone on their shoulder

I dedicate this Chapter to talk about Rescuers because I encounter them often in my life's journey. By "Rescuers", I refer to the tendency in us to take on the whole world as if they are our responsibility especially when it exceeds our limits. Rescuers would *jump into the deep end on behalf of others at the cost of their wellbeing as a persistent pattern.* They serve the vital function in stabilising or saving the grace in a rather fragile or endangered system at home, at work or in society which is valid and absolutely admirable. However, the problem is, when this becomes a pattern and is overused, it can turn into a vicious cycle with a never-ending loop. The more the Rescuers fix a problem for others, the more they have to fix, because such tendency promotes others' dependence on them after a while.

Erroneous assumption and approach

The Rescuer would give the poor the fish, instead of teaching them how to fish. Nothing is wrong in doing so, except that without learning to fish, the poor are back to ask for more fish the following day. *Whilst the Rescuers' intents and deeds are very honourable and admirable, such help is nevertheless "a Band-Aid". They fix the symptom, not the cause.*

The Rescuers tend to fix it all for everyone because deep down inside, they assume that "it has to be me that fixes the problem, because everyone else is too vulnerable. Without me, the whole world will crumble." The assumption may be full-on valid in the original context when others are truly vulnerable. However, over-rescuing others blindly ultimately deprives the poor the chance to learn to stand on their own two feet. This puts the rescued in a passive role of being dependent, lazy, vulnerable and irresponsible which often leads to "victimhood", "sense of entitlement "or "Prince and Princess Syndrome" in the long run.

By over-rescuing, we give too much, love too much, do too much, protect too much and worry too much. Consequently, we stress out and burn out too much. What is meant to be others' responsibility, lessons and consequence are now ours! We thus resent ourselves for not saying enough "no" to others. Not only do we delay others' life's learning and maturity, with burn-outs and their dependence on us, over-rescuing side-tracks us from fulfilling our top priority of self-fulfilment. It hinders our self-worth too because no one can sustain good self-view when we treat ourselves as second-class citizens by always prioritising others.

Rescuers are reinforced by our systems on many levels

Rescuer is a common role that many of us adapt due to crisis, wars or some aftermaths of some kind within our family or societal systems. Some of us adapt such a role because we are projecting our own unfulfilled needs onto our next generation. Thus, we try to give as much as possible to ensure they "have it all" nice, easy and smoothly. Others adapt the role because they believe that they "owe" the others something. It is common that upon divorce, the parents tend to feel guilty for not being able to provide their children an intact family. Over-giving and over-protecting become the means of their love expression to balance out their guilt. Others rescue a lot simply because they are ultra kind and ultra giving in their nature without a healthy boundary. Many over-rescue because they lack adequate self-esteem; taking on the extra role as a Rescuer allows them to feel better about themselves (as conditioned by the society to "justify").

In a bigger context, our religions, society and traditions also play major roles to reinforce such tendency. Rescuers are often labelled as "selfless", "self-sacrificing", "virtuous", "generous", "brave", "altruistic" or "heroic". Therefore, most of the Rescuers often see nothing wrong in doing so without realising it sets them up for self-perpetuating pitfalls.

Empowerment by addressing the cause, not the symptoms

In contrast to the above burdening, over-compromising Rescuer role, luckily there is a better way out. For example, if our children are always broke, instead of giving them the money, *we have to dig a bit deeper to address the underlying cause, rather than the symptoms*. The underlying cause can be that they spend too much, do not have a job and lack confidence to go out to seek and secure a job. They might have a hard time maintaining a job with a past unresolved trauma of being bullied in their childhood. They might have major mistrust in others and life overall to even step outside the home, due to the comfort zone of being jobless for too long. It's better that we empower them by teaching them how to budget and save money, assist them finding a job, and refer them to qualified professionals to rebuild their self-confidence and resolve their trauma of childhood bullies and to rebuild trust with discernment in relating to others. Only by doing so can our children stand on their two feet for the long run.

It's a two –way street

To empower someone, it's a two-way street. One is willing to help; and the other has to be willing to receive help. After all, *God helps those who help themselves.* Until the needed are willing to step up to do something for themselves, there is nothing we can do to force their free will other than praying for them to have such strength and willingness. Sooner or later, they will have to learn the lesson: if not the easy way; the hard way.

A healthy boundary is essential when empowering others

To empower, we have to ensure that whatever we do to help and support is within our capacity first. On the plane, in crisis, we are instructed to put the air-masks on ourselves first before reaching out to anyone! It appears selfish at the first glance. However, without ensuring that we are self-sustainable on solid ground, we can easily become "the mud-Buddha going across the river" to rescue the drowning. This is where not only we cannot effect proper rescuing, but also we are sucked into a big whirlpool beyond control. We now have two people drowning! It compounds the issue.

To love wisely, it is essential that we set a healthy boundary with a time frame for our available help. Conveying the time-limit serves to prompt the rescued to step up to be self-independent. We can also help on the ground that "the rescued demonstrate signs of self-help with their action-taking or problem-solving". This also allows us to return to our self-priorities in life after stabilising the initial crisis.

When such help is beyond our capacity or capability, we can always delegate or refer them to the community, government and professionals for further help. *When in doubts as to what degree and how to empower, it is also equally important that we use our common sense, super sense and Higher Conscience as our guides.* There is always a grace balance between our reason and heart, between our idealism and our limits. It's good to think outside the square creatively to generate empowering solutions. It is nice to reach such *balance* where we can truly rejoice in reaching out whilst maintaining a solid ground of wellbeing for ourselves.

It is said that Bill Gates donates 95% of his income annually to charity. Not only does he give away food and provides a better living environment; for the long term, he also sets up a free public educational system for the poor. This is to ensure that in the long run, they will be able to use their intelligence to solve their own problems and eventually become self-sufficient. It's an excellent example of teaching the poor how to fish rather than simply giving them the fish.

Some notes about empowerment

Much like the angels' help and support to us, whilst angels have empathy for our suffering, they do not intervene without our asking, unless there is a risk of our death before our contracted time to return Home to the other side. Their help comes in the form of hints, insights, ideas, opportunities, comfort, coincidence and alternatives outside squares. They guide us to step up with self responsibility; try-out with different actions, comfort us along with the trials and errors in the journey until we master the situation, the learning.

The angels understand that because lessons are not always easy, nothing is learnt or tackled overnight. They are patient and allow us plenty of time to go through our trial and error and *leave the decision-making and action-taking for us without jumping into the deep end for us by taking over all actions. They stay detached from the final outcomes but remain genuinely caring to our overall growth and wellbeing. They trust that in due time, we will learn from our consequences in life one way or the other.* They understand that apart from love, joy, beauty, freedom, abundance and harmony, mistakes, humility, patience, tenacity, healthy risk-taking, trust, creativity and faith are *also equally important* as part of the journey to our self-empowerment. *They understand that if they rescue too much, we'd never develop much of the above strength; it defeats the very purpose of our embarking on this physical journey.*

Three months down the road....

A good formula to differentiate whether we are being a Rescuer or an Empowerment to others is to ask ourselves that," by us using the same way of help to others, three months down the road, are they likely to show some signs of standing on their own two feet?". If the answer is "yes", congratulations, you are empowering to them. If not, you are rescuing.

Antidotes to the Rescuers

There are three antidotes for the Rescuer:

1. To remember "Everything in moderation".
2. When giving too much, consider the approach of "be cruel in order to be kind" to counterbalance.
3. When the over-rescuing has become too big a burden as evidenced by our overwhelmed feelings, resentment or depression, saying "no" firmly to the rescued with a healthy boundary is always the way to go.

Homework

Whenever you realise that you are rescuing, slow down. Think of long-term empowering strategies to engage these who ask for help. Instead of jumping into the deep ends, practise all of the above concepts and tools. Others may complain due to fears of stepping out of their comfort zone, but they will eventually come to respect your boundary and learn to step up hopefully. If not, refer them for professional or community helps immediately.

Chapter vii

Self–Loyalty as Compass and Boundary

Two suitcases to carry

The mystics say that there are 44 themes for us to master before we graduate from the Cosmic Wheel (Brown, 2001). This is when we "ascend" back to the highest plane to reunite with "the Source" again. It takes us existence after existence to master the 44 themes before we reach the maturity ready to ascend. To master these lessons, each one of us is assigned with one individual theme and one group theme along with our soul-mates and soul clan for our soul's evolvement. Some themes takes many lifetimes to master depending on how focused we are on the learning at hand. This is because we tend to get side-tracked by the ego-based power and glamour which may or may not be the themes we are here to work through. Without also paying attention to the esoteric and spiritual aspects in life for counter-balance, it slows down our soul's evolvement as we are not getting the ultimate priority right.

Self-loyalty as compass to stay on track

Since we come here to experience, express our highest definition of who we are, *it is very important that whilst we are here, we stay self-loyal to fulfil our "life's plan" which is the contract our Soul Self made before birth with our Great Universe.* Many of us are so good at playing life's games as hypnotised by the sheep-mind conditionings, that we become the slaves to the games!

The Danish existential philosopher and poet Soren Kierkegaard (1813-1855) once said, "life can only be understood backwards; but it must be lived forwards". No hindsights can be obtained until we have been through the journey. We can certainly live forwards by learning from those coming close to their death by skipping some major mistakes. One of the top regrets about life in our death beds is that we failed to act in time and missed out on life's opportunities by worrying too much about others' nay-says rather than following our inner callings. This is because *we are often conditioned to be loyal to everyone else above us!*

What the dying never regret is that they followed their inner callings even though it turned out to be disappointing or hurtful. By following our inner callings, there is always something to gain spiritually. We may not fully appreciate the lessons at the time. However, when viewing life backwards, most understand that putting aside the outcome, our soul does feel fulfilled in some way. It helps us to grow and mature somehow.

Others' compass suits them. The society's formula suits the elites. Our compass is uniquely encoded in us for us to use and follow. *Without working out our innate system uniquely made for us, whatever we create based on others' compass and formulas often does not fulfil us. Living without self-fulfilment is a very dry, lonely, and self-alienating place to be. Even if we have earned the whole world's recognition, if the achievement is a mismatch to our genuine Soul Self, the big "void" can make us feel rather empty and incomplete.*

In my youth, my father used to raise pigeons as a hobby. His pigeons often won championships for different races across Taiwan. My father never ceased to marvel at how intelligent they were. Despite never exploring any new territory hundreds of kilometres away, it did not matter where they were dropped off, they'd always find their way home back to us! I believe that innate in the pigeons, there is a compass (biologically and instinctively) that guide them where they are meant to go. Like the pigeons, when we trust and utilise that innate part of us more often, we can achieve and be self-fulfilled far better.

Seven energy centres

My Godfather the late Dr. Jon Young, N.D. from Hawaii often said to me that our Universe is clever in reminding us who we are by creating the rainbows. This is because when observing our human energy field, there are seven energy centres (the seven chakras) inside us that emit the same colours coinciding with the rainbow. From the base chakra all the way up to the crown chakra, it goes in the colour order of the rainbow spectrum: red, orange, yellow, green, blue, violet and purple.

Self-loyalty affects our wellbeing on all levels

The seven chakras connect with our physical, emotional, mental and spiritual functioning. When we do our moment-to-moment decision-making, we either honour our real divine self or we deny it. It is the "I am that I am" (our Higher Self or Soul Self) that envelops our human body. As emphasized earlier, we are truly spiritual beings having physical human experiences.

Much like the movie "Avatar", when we embark on this physical journey, we are taking a fraction of our Higher Soul's energy to project it into this physical reality for our experience and expression. Whilst we are here, we remain in touch with our Home Base on the Higher Spiritual realm. The projected us here in this three dimensional reality is always connected with our Higher Self on the Home Base. When we choose to ignore our inner callings (usually through our energy alignment to the seven Chakras which will bring on sharpening of our intuition), we can get lost easily in this myriad of physical reality. On the contrary, when we tune into our guidance, and align with the chakras inside us and heed accordingly, we are more likely to have clarity and live a more balanced, fulfilled and joyous life.

Self-loyalty starts with slowing down our "yes" to others

The maintenance of our self-loyalty depends on our daily decision makings throughout our life spans. *Every decision we make leads to some consequences. Many of them have impacts on generations to come.* When the first African American woman refused to sit at the back seat of the bus as an expression to her entitled equal rights as a human, that simple decision alone decades ago has sparked a whole chain of social movements for racial and gender equality in the U.S.A.

Whilst saying "yes" to others and the authority are conditioned by the society as if it's a "virtue" because it shows our "agree-ability" and willingness to "conformity" and "support", over-use "yes" to others blindly without matching it to our Soul Self's true desire, can lead to us being "dis-eased" with our true self within. Over time, with such self-denial of going against the every grain of what we are made, the compounded self-denial and self-negation can create "diseases".

Premature "yes" means no one is standing on our ground

For those of us that are too kind, too soft, too selfless and too self-sacrificing, it is important that we slow down our "yes" to others' requests especially when being "put on the spot" to make a decision. Each person has his or her own ground, and when we say "yes" too soon too fast to support the others' ground, it leaves no one standing on our ground. This leaves us in a very difficult situation because to exit a lousy deal we impulsively say yes to will take ten times the efforts for us to bail out.

Instead of saying "yes" to every request automatically without considering our own grounds, it is wise for us to say "I am not sure: let me think about it. I will get back to you in ____ time". This will alleviate the pressure immediately. By doing so, we are not offending anyone except for demonstrating that we do have sincere effort to think over it deeper. During such time out, we can refocus *on attending to the 7 aspects of our life correlating with our 7 chakras for sound decision-making towards better self-fulfilment.*

7 Major questions for self-loyal decision making

The following 7 questions are what we go through as a checklist for our daily and significant decision-making to stay self-loyal. Please answer "yes" or "no" alongside each question. When in doubt, it's always a "no".

"If I were to agree to this situation or request:"

1. Does it support my "needs" for securing my basic survival, money and job? ____ (Y/ N)

The base chakra is located at the base of our spine, orbiting in clear red colour in the shape of a flower or funnel stretching out. It governs our physical, material needs of survival such as our money, job or anything concerning our physical safety and security.

If our boss threatens to fire us upon our refusal and we have not much savings in the bank to get by immediately to sustain our livelihood, then we "need" the job (whether we like it or not). Needing something means "without such, we'd be in big trouble of having no roof above us, no food on the table and no money to provide the basic physical and material safety and security".

2. Does it give me what I "desire" or "want"? ___(Y/N)

The second chakra is at our naval, orbiting in clear orange colour, governing our physical/material wants, desires and creativity.

To differentiate: "needs" are essential, without such, we cannot sustain or survive physically and financially; "wants" are bonus, and it gives us "pleasure". Without pleasure, we still survive.

3. Does it support my innate "power" as an equal person? or Am I getting a fairshare in return to maintain my self-authority, self-confidence and respect? ___(Y/N)

The third chakra, is located at our solar plexus which is below our diaphragm and above our naval. It rotates in clear yellow colour, governing our power and control issues in life for self-esteem and self-confidence. This is where "50/50" principle runs. When we give 50% of who we are; to maintain the equality and healthy equilibrium, we need to receive 50% back in return.

Much like our breathing: we breathe in to receive, so that we can breathe out to give. Likewise, we breathe out to give, so that we can make space to breathe in to receive. We can get into trouble easily by breathing in or breathing out excessively without equal exchange. It's when we have equal exchange with the outside world that we will sustain our life with a nice and easy flow resulting with wellbeing.

Giving too much shows low self-worth and it depletes us. Taking too much shows insecurity for which we are not capable of accommodating either. Either way, we get sucked into the power game of being undermined or being too dominant and selfabsorbed. *Abundance favours where the energy free flows.*

4. In my meditative clear state, do I "feel" good about this? ___(Y/N)

The fourth chakra locates on our heart area. It orbits in the colour of emerald green and light pink. It governs our physical and emotional healing with unconditional love. To align with our true "feeling", we need to put aside the "should" and "have to" and others' opinions or influences and remain still in our *meditative state (which is a calm and clear state achieved through deep breathing and relaxing). Then we ask:* "what's my first impression, gut feeling or intuition or bodily reaction in my heart area? If my heart feels "good", "uplifted", "warm" or "euphoric", this is a good indication that you are on the "right track". The answer to this chakra is "yes". If not, it is a "no". If it is a mixture of "good "and "bad" feelings: it is still a "no" when in doubt. We are better off saying "no" first to allow us the right to negotiate for better terms and conditions before we say "yes" to it.

5. Does it support my truth, value or belief system?___(Y/N)

The fifth chakra is located at our throat area. It orbits in the colour of turquoise which governs our speech, representing our truth, values and belief system. This is where we say what we mean and then we mean what we say with actions for integrity. If the presented request supports our inner truth, value and belief, the answer is "yes" to this chakra; if not, it is a "no".

6. Does it support my "vision"?___(Y/N)

The sixth chakra is located at the centre of our forehead above our eyebrows. It orbits the colour of violet blue and governs our "inner vision". Our inner vision represents the big picture, our purpose and meaning. If our vision is to be a "humanitarian" of some form, being offered a big career working for a crook just to make top dollars does not support our bigger picture in life. The answer to this question in this chakra would be a "no".

If the big vision of our life is to be a musician, being offered a big pay as a car salesman does not match our inner vision; unless the money we earn from selling cars serves the purpose to pay towards the tuition fees to become one.

7. Does it support my "inner knowing" or "higher conscience" that the decision covers the wellbeing for all?

The seventh chakra is located on the crown area. It orbits in the colour of purple colour. It governs our inner direct higher knowing that everything and everyone in this Universe is connected as one. Since we are connected as one, what goes around comes around. Therefore, to support our inner knowing, our "yes" has to support both "our highest good", and "the highest good of all". If not, it is a "no".

For example, by saying "yes" to drug-dealing, it is supporting our good of paying off all our debts and paying towards the big mansion we have always wanted, but it is not for our "highest" good (since the drug–dealing puts us at the high risk of jail terms) and it is not for the "highest" good for our communities because the drugs will destroy many individuals and families' lives for generations to come. It is a "no" to this question.

The more self-loyal, the more aligned we are with our Soul Self

The more we can say "yes" to the above 7 questions internally to match coherently with our "yes" to others externally, the more fulfilling and aligned we are to our Soul Self with our decision making. However, if there is any "no "to any of the 7 questions:

1. We need to slow down and do problem–solving within ourselves to resolve our inner conflicts amongst all the chakras to have a happy ending for all chakras involved.

2. We can also use our no's on the list to negotiate with the outside world for better terms and conditions to create a win/win outcome for all involved. This is where we say "If I scratch your back, you can scratch mine too". The no's in our chakra list means that there are yet some things for us to address first, and that unless the other parties are willing to co-create a win/win solution for us, in general, we are better off moving on elsewhere with a "no". If we cannot do so immediately for other priorities involved, when the timing is better with change of circumstances, we can still come back to fulfil this chakra better as feasible.

So saying, I am not pushing for fulfilling the higher ends of chakras blindly by compromising the 3 lower chakras either. Being spiritual and idealistic does not mean that we should ignore our physical and material needs for survival and self-sufficiency. If by pursuing a dream (which entails our higher chakras' passion, values, visions and altruism), we are risking becoming penniless, jobless and homeless immediately, it is not a sound decision!

It is important that we weigh the risks involved whenever we are making the efforts to balance out different aspects of our life associated with our 7 chakras. A sensible approach will be to slow down and plan things out better to ensure the transitions are smooth without creating unnecessary trauma and dramas. This is particularly important when we have children's wellbeing under our care to consider. If we are stuck with an unhappy job (base and second chakras) that gives us stable income but not fulfilling (the higher end chakras), we may want to keep the job for the time being until we can secure our next job that is more satisfying and fulfilling for the long run.

On the other hand, we might be equally miserable with an unhappy job that fulfils our base chakra with lots of money but without any passion, value nor visions derived from it. For example, a person's heart desire is to be a singer (heart chakra) but also wants to own a big house (base chakra energy) at the same time. His big house requires a stable and excellent income. However, working as a singer does not provide him sufficient income for his big mortgage. If he wants to have a win/ win solution, he either has to be happy with a smaller house whilst keeping his job as a singer until such time when he can earn a bigger income. Alternatively, he can compromise his privacy by co-sharing his big house with a few tenants to keep both his desired job and house at the same time. He can consider working 2 or 3 jobs to keep up with his mortgage payments. However, being overly exhausted from taking on too many jobs may jeopardise his base chakras as the burn-outs will threaten his physical wellbeing. By generating a win/ win solution to create a balance for all chakras involved, the person will be happier and more fulfilled rather than feeling stuck with an unhappy job only to live in a big house in misery.

I know many of such examples where *"one owns the whole world (lower 3 chakras), but loses their heart and soul (top 4 chakras)"*. Many turn to alcohol, drugs, gambling, excessive work, sex and greed as means of filling up the "emptiness" within for escape. However, none of these escapes will bring them true joy or fulfilment.

Sometimes we slip into our comfort zone after making some initial over-compromise to ignore certain chakras within us, only to realise years later that we have been stuck in a rather unhappy situation for too long. The above check list is equally helpful for both the immediate situations at hand and the overall life review for better decision-makings.

To illustrate, let's say the same man above has chosen to quit his singing job and worked hard as a construction manager for 25 years because he has 3 children to feed. He is now a middle-aged man and he does have a big home but he is indifferent to his job but has continued yearning to be a musician. By reviewing the chart, there is an unfulfilled aspect which relates to his heart chakra which is his true passion in life. Realising so, it's a matter of problem-solving to attend to his heart's desire with concrete actions. Nothing stops him from fulfilling his original passion and vision by forming a band of his own with a few like-minded musicians in his community now that he is financially secured and relatively carefree with children already being independent. Nothing stops him from creating his own music,or run his own meet-up group. Better yet, he can travel afar in different regions annually as wished. When this can be done, it is usually very uplifting to our spirit! Don't be surprised that when we honour our inner calling to align with who we genuinely are, how much amazing support we receive from "the other side"!!

Finally, it is important that we learn to say "no" *lovingly, firmly and persistently* to the "nay-says" from others for fulfilling all aspects of who we are eventually. It's never too late to be happy.

Homework

This Chapter is about making a deliberate choice to live a self-loyal, and self-authentic life that is balanced in all aspects for self-fulfilment in the best way we can. It takes efforts to practise such. *The check-list is not a "must" each time, but for important decision making, it is a good guide for creating more soulful and hearty results.*

Chapter viii

The Magic Touch for Creation

Originating from our Great Creator, we are also great creators: our innate divine nature is to create. Because mastering the art of creation is one of the major learnings in our soul evolvement, I am writing this Chapter to share "the magic touch" on creation. Our human conditionings often teach us to use our "brain" to think, to decide and to rule our life. There is no doubt that our intellect has played a very influential role in our modern evolution in the last three centuries. However, when it comes to materialising our intent for creation, a more effective way is to follow our heart and soul which play a far more significant role than our head in "the Law of Manifestation". It is essential that we engage both our heart and head for manifestation.

The secret is in our heart

Our modern science has discovered that the magnetic energy field around our heart chakra is actually five thousand times stronger than what is surrounding our brain area (Braddon, 2006). Our heart chakra is the centre where the lower three chakras (the base, navel and solar plexus) meet with the higher three chakras (the throat, the 3rd eye and the crown chakra). It is the energy meeting-point of the six major chakras within our etheric body.

Interestingly, in most mystic teachings, it is well known that our Higher-Self communicates with us through our "heart", not our "head"! Whilst our head is being conditioned to have its habitual automatic responses with ongoing chit-chats (which feature our usual fear-based ego), it is our heart that receives direct impressions from our Soul Self. Therefore, in meditation, we are often taught to quiet our mind and focus on just being in the present with deep breathing, whilst gently releasing the chit-chats.

In many ancient Chinese metaphysical and Buddhists' teachings, it is often encouraged that we "practise being soulful" for approaching any tasks at hand in order to be "better-focused" in life. In other words, they have since thousands of years ago the understanding that by linking our intellect to our soul, we can achieve more effective and fulfilled outcomes.

Emotions create powerful energy vortex for manifestation

When our repeated thoughts emit powerful emotional states such as love, joy, passion, faith, enthusiasm, determination etc., we are actually engaging our cosmic energy much like creating a "vortex" where our manifestation suddenly intensifies and accelerates **(Hicks, Esther & Jerry, 2009). Such is the secret to the magic touch in creation.**

To sum up about the magic touch to manifestation, basically, it is crucial to know that:

1. Everything in this universe vibrates its unique frequency. From a pebble, to a dog, to vitamin B, to a papaya tree, to a dragonfly, to John Cleese, to Marilyn Monroe in fact every living being vibrates. Not only that, every thought, every feeling, every word, every emotion, every image, every sound, every colour, everything that exists has its own signatory vibration.

2. All vibration is electro-magnetically charged, which means that it is "attractive" in its nature.

3. Like attracts like. Birds of the same feather flock together.

   "As within, so without". The energy or vibes we emit from our thoughts and emotions within us always attract their matched events, situations and people in our external world. If we believe that we are not worthy, it's not a surprise that we attract people, events and circumstances that match our belief of being unworthy. If we feel really lucky, it's no coincidence that we win a big lotto that makes us feel very fortunate!

4. When there are any doubts in our intent and fears in our emotions, our manifestation slows down: it's like three steps forward but two steps back. *To improve manifestation, it's important to work through deeply ingrained negative emotional patterns to release them. Doing so makes manifestation of what we want in life easier to manifest. When releasing the trauma -induced negative patterns becomes too challenging, it is wise to seek timely professional help.*

5. Emotions vary on different frequencies on a continuum. They range from the lowest vibes of guilt and shame, despair, unworthiness, fears and doubts to the highest end of love, joy, truth, freedom, passion, gratitude, peace and abundance. It's important to find the "slightly better" emotion as the "next immediate" goal to aim at for easier manifestation. For example, if one is in grief and despair, to be fully joyous immediately is very difficult due to the huge vibrational gap between the two emotions. To shift from despair, one is better off starting out with replacing it with "anger" or "blames", before moving onto "disappointments" to "pessimism" followed by cultivation of

"content" before moving towards "hopefulness", to "positive expectation" of life to "passion" and then "joy".

6. Gratitude and willingness to accept our ups and downs as part of our soulful learnings in life make the moving of the above vibrational scale easier.

7. Since everything is about vibration and frequency, to manifest effectively, it is important to make deliberate and conscious choices habitually in our daily routines. They include what we watch, listen to, eat, drink, talk, attend to, think, feel and act. Whatever we focus on repeatedly over time affects our core beliefs and our emotional states which affect the manifestation of our reality. *By making deliberate and conscious efforts on what we choose and what we want, we manifest more effectively what we truly intend and desire.*

8. Positive affirmation, visualisation and genuine giving of what we want to others (without asking anything in return) helps to accelerate manifestation.

"Happy go lucky" for effortless manifestation

When we observe little children before they download too much human conditionings, they are happy naturally. They simply "are" happy without having to own a big house or become influential. They simply are joyous without having to impress anyone. It is a natural state of our divine essence in its natural expression. The criteria for being happy with "doing" and "having" are man-made concepts. We don't have to postpone our being happy until "when I find a good husband", or "when I have a Ferrari" or "when I finally lose 10 kilos". We can choose to be happy now very deliberately to counteract our conditionings. Happiness is a high vibrational state of being, from which we attract the higher ends of opportunities, good fortune and abundance naturally, thus the famous saying of "happy go lucky".

Acceptance and allowing

It is challenging for us to be happy when we are undergoing some hardship in life. So saying, *dwelling on the negatives will only attract more of the same low vibes which eventually will materialise as a self-fulfilled prophecy. Upon such, we will say, "see, I was right"!*

To break through such a vicious cycle, it is very important for us to "make peace with the circumstances by acceptance with self-responsibility." In Emerging out of Cocoon (Hsieh, 2015), the author's Inner God explains that acceptance means "if life gives us lemons, turn them into lemonade."

Gratitude boosts manifestation

Gratitude is a form of love, which is the highest vibe in this universe. If we cannot come up with a good feeling immediately, we can start by counting our little blessings moment to moment, to build up the momentum of feeling good. For example, instead of worrying about job loss, we are better off refocusing on how lucky we are with other forms of safety and security that are already in our life.

This is because somewhere not far away in the local hospital, someone is battling to live after major surgery; somewhere 30 hours away by flight, millions of decent civilians like us are facing political crisis where their homeland has become a war zone overnight. Instead of enjoying decent and basic daily safe and clean living, they are now roaming around in the cold with no country to go to, nor tomorrow to look forward to. We have a lot to be thankful where we are. It's a matter of practise.

Focus on "why" and "what", rather than "how"

Every creation is a co-creation with our Great Universe. With our "inner parallel universe" as the origin of our creation (Hsieh, 2015), it is important to understand that as powerful creators ourselves, our role is to focus on "why" (the intent) we desire what we desire, and "what" it is that we desire. It's the Great Universe's job to come up with the "how" to match with "why" and "what" we want (Hicks, 2009). *Whenever we focus on "how" we can manifest, our vibration goes down because we have no control about who, and what, where, and when and how things are going to unfold along the way, once we shoot out our intents. However, by focusing on "why" and "what" we desire, it boosts our passion and clarity to accelerate the creation process.*

The more altruistic the intent, the greater the support for manifestation

Whilst emotions hold powerful energy vortex to our manifestation, our intent settings are equally crucial. There are 3 levels of intents which engage with different levels of energy support from the Universe:

1. The personal material intent: this usually include intents for our personal material possessions, houses, money and career. With this level of intent, we attract the lowest amount of support for manifestation.

2. Intent for personal growth: this covers intents for personal, ancestral transformation on the mental, emotional and metaphysical level. For example with intent to transform "I can't" attitude, "poor me", "the tall poppy syndrome"

or "power and control tendency", we receive bigger team support from the other side for manifestation.

3. The altruistic intent for benefitting community and humanity or our eco system: this is where our intent is for "the highest good of all" on the collective level. Setting up an eco-friendly "recycle centre" with the intent of re-engineering and re-welding unwanted bikes into usable wheelchairs for the disabled in the less developed countries to use for free is a good example for this level of manifestation! With this level of intent, we attract various Archangels and Ascended Masters in addition to our whole team of angel guidance as support to join us for powerful and grander co-creation to benefit humanity!

Heaven on Earth is obtainable via alignment within

In addition to the above Law of Manifestation, yoga and meditation practice are another powerful means of manifestation. The New Age mystic Drunvalo Melchizedek teaches that in Kriya and Kundalini yoga, by linking our pineal gland to our 3rd eye and pituitary gland in meditation, we can bypass the influences of our polarized brains to connect with our Soul Self (our innate compass) for creating "heaven on earth" without the manifestation of unwanted polarity (Melchizedek, 1999).

Homework

With the above in mind, in our daily life, put aside 15 to 30 minutes' time in a meditative state to just "be". Be happy, if we want to attract happiness. Be content and abundant, if we want attract content and abundance. Be at peace with ourselves, if we want peace and harmony in our outside world. Whatever we want, be it first to attract the opportunities for us to do and act upon. With such, we will have it.

Empathy and Non-Judgement Compassion

"The purpose of human life is to serve,
and to show compassion, and the will to help others."
— *Albert Schweitzer*

The angels often say that if only we have a bit more empathy and compassion for our other human fellows, we'd advance far faster as an individual and a species. This is because they "know" that we are utterly "one". We are in this humanity for our learning and evolvement together. We are all brothers and sisters that come from the same Origin. We would not do anything harmful to our own biological families, so why would we do anything harmful to our soul family? Doing so is much like getting our right arm to cut off our left arm. Such acts are unthinkable! We do so to one another because we are not recognising that the so-called "them" are "us" from the Collective Consciousness point of view.

There is no one but God, there is nothing but Love (Robert, 1994)

Some of us have been subject to pastlife and after-life regression hypnotherapies to unlock our deep subconscious and unconscious memories of our past existences across time and dimensions. To sum up, we are literally "gods" and "goddesses" containing tons of sacred jewel within us. In each one of our existences here or in other galaxies, we polish a whole different set of sacred jewels each time. We help each other out by taking turns to play different roles and stories on life's different stages for our evolvement. Ultimately, everything in life is a delusion; only love is real. Everyone looks separate from each other, but it's an illusion; there is only one of us, which is the Unity of all of us, God.

The truth is all of us have been male and female, saints and criminals, prestigious and nobody, the judge and the judged, the villain and the victims, the heroes and the cowards. prostitutes and saints.. Each role in every context teaches our soul something that further defines the unique individuality of who we are as souls. Therefore, chances are that the very cultures or roles or identities or situations we judge and look down upon in this lifetime are likely to be the very ones we have lived and gone through in our past existences. We simply have "memory amnesia" that wipes out our past for the sake of keeping us "focused" on our new role and identity to extract the best learning out of it. The very cultures and race we hate can be the very places we will incarnate into in the future because our "bias" now requires readjustment and balance. Understanding this Higher Truth prevents us from being arrogant, judgemental and discriminative whilst we harbour deep compassion and empathy instead.

Doing unto the others is doing unto us

It is therefore unthinkable and a nonsense to judge or treat others unkindly with ego-centralism or ethno-centralism, because judging others literally is judging ourselves. Albert Einstein once said, "The world will not be destroyed by those who do evil, but by those who watch them without doing anything..... our task must be to free ourselves from this prison by widening our circle of compassion to embrace all living creatures and the whole of nature in its beauty." It seems that the highly evolved intelligent beings have the common understanding of how important it is to extend our loving, caring and empathic parts of who we are beyond our immediate family if we are to survive and evolve well as a species, as a collective whole.

We would not get our nose to remove our mouth, just so that our whole body is full of nose to breathe, but no mouth to speak nor teeth to chew. We would not get our hands to cut out our stomach and large intestines, just so that our body can move around with too many hands like octopuses but have nothing left to digest the nutrients or eliminate the waste! It would be a disaster. Different ethnic background and culture contribute uniquely to our humanity as a whole, much like different organs play different roles to serve our collective whole; removing any or condemning any would be disastrous. The same principle applies on the person to person interpersonal level.

In life-review, we get to taste our own medicine

Some souls do not have much empathy nor compassion for others whilst being alive. They live like "walking zombies" as conditioned by man-made values. As universally revealed in tons of documented transpersonal regression sessions, we all have to go through Life Review when we make it to the other side after we die. This is where every deed we have ever had since our birth to the moment we die is replayed like a film being rewound.

In the life review, there is no judgement nor judge but our own Soul Self who reviews our own deeds for soul evolvement. What we give with our deeds, we are made to feel the very impacts we have created on the other side. This is not designed for "punishment" or any derogatory reason but for the sake of promoting the soul's innate "empathy" and "compassion".

Walking in others' shoes as means of growing

It is not unusual that if we stubbornly refuse to empathise with others we mistreat, our Higher Soul would agree to walk in the very shoes of those who we have "judged" and "mistreated". This is to accelerate our soul's evolvement whilst balancing our deeds. Literally, we are placed in the receiving end of our own deeds "to taste our own medicine". For that reason, *whilst we are alive on this physical planet, it is always nice to remember our big picture of who we are with empathy and non-judgement compassion when we deal with others who are in need of help, love and support.*

When in crisis, or distressed life-and- death or refugee state, if this is us that experience the scenario, wouldn't we all want to be rescued, loved and supported? Wouldn't we all want to be given the chance for a place to stay for safety, security, cleanliness and comfort? Wouldn't we all want to be treated with respect? Wouldn't it be nice that we are given the opportunity to blend in and stand on our own two feet for self-reliance and self–sufficiency for our dignity?

Empathy and compassion

Whilst empathy is a state of being by resonating and tuning in to how others are feeling and experiencing, compassion is more like an action to express such empathic feelings by rendering to others a sense of wellbeing with benevolence and kind acts.

If there is a big rock on the road where someone tripped over and was severely injured with a broken leg, empathy in us would generate the very emotions of feeling identical to the injured *as if it's happening to us.* Our compassion would prompt us to call the ambulance whilst reassuring the wounded with comfort and support. Our empathy and compassion make us "do *unto others as we would have them do unto us*" as well as "avoid *doing unto others as we would not have them do unto us*". Such feeling and action state are signs of divine intelligence common to all highly evolved species.

What goes around, comes around

I was once invited as a guest speaker to 30 children to talk about how we inter-affect each other on the energy level. When I randomly handpicked one little boy to say harsh words towards another boy across the room, to his very surprise, when I pressed around his wrist his muscle strength dropped instantly. The boy who received such harsh words also dropped his muscle strength. When I asked the same little boy to send love and give genuine compliments, both of their muscle strengths became rock-solid instantly. *Energy-wise, we cannot get away from what we give out. Whatever we give, we must have it ourselves, and we become it, even though our intent is aiming towards others.*

The loving benevolence energy field attracts the highest vibes

In my spiritual quest for understanding Life, one of the best true stories I have ever come across is the example set by the Chinese scholar called Mr Yuan, Liao-Fan in the Ming Dynasty several hundred years ago. He was well-known for his writing of "Liao-Fan's Four Major Commitments" which was treated as a family bible for all his children, and descendants for many generations. In his four Commitments, he literally role-modelled and required that all his family clans go out to do three small acts of kindness and compassion deliberately daily to the community as a habit however small they were. It was not a surprise how quickly this became a "culture" within his family.

It was observed that with dedicated practise of such philosophy and kind acts within his family clan, without deliberately pursuing any materialistic, political, educational or social achievements, for many generations to come after his death, his family clans have produced hundreds of outstanding and reputable prominent decendents that were well-loved and well-respected in the fields mentioned above in their local communities. I am sure there are many beautiful examples of the same across cultures around the globe. This is just to show that when we give freely without the intent of getting anything back, we receive generous rewards by our Universe tenfold in return!

Healing and evolving faster together

If only we all can self-role-model and educate our children from a young age to have empathy and compassion for others in need, our whole world can really heal and evolve faster! We are in this big vessel of "Humanity" together. Wouldn't it be amazing if we can all see the light in each other and be the light for each other?! Wouldn't it be sensational if we all can awaken to our true divine identity as Gods and Goddesses within, and express our infinite sacred jewel within to help out our global community the best we can? Many of us are the very souls returning from the Atlantis and Lemurian era to assist the transformation of humanity to 5D reality. Here we are again millions of years later to round up our learning better. Such is the grace of the Great Universe for us: we are given time and time again to try out, until we get it right.

The time is now! May our journey be fully blessed and filled with bliss!

Namaste!!

Homework

Every day, have deliberate loving intentions with 3 little kind acts to be the channel of blessings to those we encounter. They can be giving the language of love, praise, encouragement, support or appreciation; prayers for others in need; or compassionate acts to help out our local or global communities whether they are humans or other living species. It is important to **stay detached** *from being "rewarded" or "being recognised". True giving asks nothing in return.*

References

Andrews, Andy The Butterfly Effect: How Your Life Matters, Thomas Nelson, 2010.

Braddon, Gregg The Divine Matrix: Bridging Time, Space, Miracles and Belief, Hay House, 2006.

Browne, Sylvia and Harrison, Lindsay The Other Side and Back: A Psychic's Guide to Our World and Beyond, New American Library, 2000.

Capra, Fritjof The Tao of Physics: An Exploration of the Parallels between Modern Physics and Eastern Mysticism, 3rd edition, Harper Collins, 1992.

Capra, Fritjof and Luisi, Pier Luigi The Systems View of Life: A Unifying Vision, Cambridge University Press, 2019.

Coll, Francisco The Real You: Discover Your True Life Purpose, Americana Leadership Press, 2007.

Hand Clow,Barbara The Pleiadian Agenda: A New Cosmology for the Age of Light, Bear Company, 1995.

Hicks, Esther and Hicks, Jerry The Vortex: Where the Law of Attraction Assembles All Cooperative Relationships, Hay House, 2009.

Hieh, Ming-Jieh Emerging out of Cocoon (as translated from its Chinese title), Sang Zhou Press, 2015.

Lanphear, Roger Unified: Course on Truth and Practical Guidance from Babaji, Devorss & Co., 2nd revised edition, 1988.

Lipton, Bruce The Biology of Belief: Unleashing the Power of Consciousness, Matter & Miracles, Hay House, 2015.

Martin, Joel and Romanowski, Patricia, We Don't Die: George Anderson's Conversations with the Other Side, Penguin Putnam, 2003.

Melchizdek, Drunvalo the Ancient Secret of the Flower of Life, vol, 1, Light Technology, 1999.

Roberts, Jane, Seth Speaks: The Eternal Validity of the Soul, New World Library, 1994.

San Mao, Three Hairs The Story of the Sahara (as translated from its Chinese title), Royal Crown Publishing, 1976.

Tipping, Colin C. Radical Forgiveness: Making Room for the Miracle, 2nd edition, Golden 13 Publications, 2002.

Walsch, Neale Donald, Conversations with God, book IV: Awaken the Species: A New and Unexpected Dialogue, Watkins Publishing, 2018.

Wilde, Stuart, The Quickening, Revised Edition, Hay House, 2011.

Yogananda, Paramahansa, Autobiography of a Yogi, Ancient Wisdom Publications, 2019.

List of Painting

To order Li-Ing Wu's paintings, please visit:

www.sacredjewelwithin.com

About the Author

Li-Ing (pronounced as "Lee Ing", meaning "Beautiful Shining Jade") Wu is a humanitarian. She has worked for and supported humanity for more than twenty years. From a young age she has been on a spiritual quest with the passion to understand and uplift humanity. Born and raised in Taiwan, coupled with her journey West to America and Australia, she has been  well exposed to various metaphysical heritages including Taoism, Buddhism, Naturalism, Existentialism and many New Age esoteric teachings.

Observing our global crisis at hand, Li-Ing wishes to help humanity by sharing many of her intuited spiritual insights along with simple hands-on tools to assists us to bridge our head with our heart; our human-conditioned ego with our Soul Self to live a happier and more fulfilling life.

Li-Ing lives in Australia. She enjoys a simple life with her friends and family.